"WHEN YOU think straig... but pushing ... ... at the same time. Are you?"

"Me?" She gasped, as if the thought were outrageous.

He saw right through her. "I'm right, aren't I?" He narrowed his eyes, his gaze like a laser piercing the walls of protection she counted on, then slid his hand into her hair.

"You're wrong," she insisted. "You don't know a thing about me."

"Let's fix that. Right now," he whispered, his breath warm on her lips.

She swayed toward him slightly, even as warning lights flashed behind her eyes. Danger! Danger! He was supposed to back off, stay on his side of the line, but instead she felt them both sliding toward the edge. . . .

WHAT ARE *LOVESWEPT* ROMANCES?

They are stories of true romance and touching emotion. We believe those two very important ingredients are constants in our highly sensual and very believable stories in the LOVE-SWEPT line. Our goal is to give you, the reader, stories of consistently high quality that may sometimes make you laugh, sometimes make you cry, but are always fresh and creative and contain many delightful surprises within their pages.

Most romance fans read an enormous number of books. Those they truly love, they keep. Others may be traded with friends and soon forgotten. We hope that each LOVESWEPT romance will be a treasure—a "keeper." We will always try to publish

LOVE STORIES YOU'LL NEVER FORGET BY AUTHORS YOU'LL ALWAYS REMEMBER

The Editors

Loveswept ® 748

DREAM LOVER

ADRIENNE STAFF

For Kathleen —
Hugs & love !
Adrienne

BANTAM BOOKS
NEW YORK · TORONTO · LONDON · SYDNEY · AUCKLAND

DREAM LOVER
A Bantam Book / July 1995

If you would be interested in receiving protective vinyl covers for your
Loveswept books, please write to this address for information:

Loveswept
Bantam Books
P.O. Box 985
Hicksville, NY 11802

ISBN 0-553-44351-8

Published simultaneously in the United States and Canada

PRINTED IN THE UNITED STATES OF AMERICA

OPM   0 9 8 7 6 5 4 3 2 1

PROLOGUE

A man was running across the hilltop, a bare, beautiful man racing against a red sky. His body was gleaming with sweat, the muscles rippling across his chest and back, the long, hard muscles of his thighs tightening and stretching with every swift stride. His hair was black as night, a wild mane flying behind him. His heart was pounding, as if every evil in the world were chasing at his heels. Fleet-footed, he reached the edge of the cliff . . . and yet he ran on, magically leaping up into the sky, his body transforming from muscle and flesh to feather and talon. He was an eagle, dark and powerful, soaring against the endless blue. And she . . . she was left far below, a small figure wandering through a maze of old ruins. In the dimness she bumped against a cold stone wall, stumbled on the crumbled rocks covered in the dust of centuries. But she couldn't leave. She was searching for something, something she'd lost so long ago. She was weeping, her heart broken. When she fell, she could not get up again. Then an old man appeared, an old Indian in a ceremonial robe with feathers and beads, bits of glass sewn on the buckskin. She saw herself reflected there in a hundred tiny mirrors, each image shattered. He reached for her, and it was as if she could hear the words: "Stand. Take off your jacket. Take off your dress, your shoes. Untie your hair. Stand, and take off your skin, your bones, your sorrow. Take the stone out of your heart. Here . . ." His palm lay open. "Place it in my hand." But she was too frightened, her arms and hands weighted down with fear. Her body was paralyzed, her feet had taken root. Yet suddenly she was balanced at the very edge of the cliff; there was only air and sky behind her, and the old man moving toward her, closer and closer, his hands outstretched. This time he chanted aloud words that her heart somehow understood: *To fly with the eagle is to reach for the stars.* And then his hand touched her—

"No! No, stop! Don't push me!"

Carol Lawson sat bolt upright in bed, her heart pounding, her body wet with a cold sheen of sweat. She took a deep gulp of air and pressed her hand to her breasts, struggling to shake off the last strands of the dream that clung to her eerily. It had been so vivid, so real, so contradictory. She knew all too well that heartbreaking sense of loss, that grief she'd lived with so long. The pictures in the dream were terrifying: Herself lost and searching amidst places and things she'd never seen or even imagined before.

She lay back down and pulled the covers up to her chin, a storm of emotions sweeping through her. Somehow the strange dream had opened a door to the old, terrible sadness, reminding her of a part of her life that she usually was able to keep deeply hidden, even from herself. But mixed with the fear and grief was an unexplainable excitement. There'd been *magic* in that dream, frightening her, but thrilling her too. How had *her* subconsious ever concocted such a wild and powerful vision? What did it mean?

Hugging herself, Carol searched for a sensible answer and found it in the moving boxes and suitcases piled around her bedroom. Anyone would be upset the night before starting a new job, a new life. That's all it was; that's all it meant. But even as she closed her eyes, her thoughts leapt ahead to the desert Southwest and what might be waiting there.

ONE

"Don't touch that! Don't touch a damn thing," growled a deep voice from the dark corner of the lobby.

Carol stepped back quickly from the display of Indian artifacts she'd paused to admire.

The hotel lobby of the Ocotillo was almost empty at midnight, with the exception of the night clerk doing paperwork behind the front desk. The faint sound of a native flute came from the same shadowy corner as the voice, music so lyrical and mystical, it seemed to transform the quiet lobby into the far reaches of the desert itself.

Carol waited expectantly, peering past the glass cases into the darkness. Finally she shrugged. "Hello? I'm sorry. I was just trying to get a closer look."

"Don't. It's closer looks and careless hands that destroy these ancient things." As he spoke, a man emerged from the shadows, parting the darkness that surrounded him. He was tall, lean, and ruggedly handsome in worn jeans and cowboy boots, the kind of man you had to look at twice. Riveting. Perhaps a bit dangerous. His eyes were masked by the darkness of the room, but Carol could feel him looking at her; she felt his gaze slide over her and linger like a touch.

Her whole body tightened, and for a second she felt something mysterious take hold of her—a jolt of emotion. But was it excitement, fear, or . . . recognition? She actually took a half step forward, her heart fluttering, before she caught herself and stopped, confused by her response to this absolute stranger.

He frowned, and narrowed his eyes warily as he looked into the blue depths of her eyes and saw his own pain and hunger mirrored there. His heart clenched in his chest. What had he seen? Who was this woman? But in an instant he became stone again, cold and distant. "I'll be done in an hour. Come back then."

Lifting her chin, she said, "I may if I have time. I'm the new assistant manager. I came in to do a little paperwork. I didn't mean to bother you."

"Good."

She frowned. "Do you work for the hotel?"

"Occasionally." Coldly he turned his back and placed a long hunting bow on the shelf next to a quiver of arrows.

"That's beautiful," Carol said, giving it one more try. "The whole display looks fascinating. Is it owned by the hotel or on loan from—?"

"There'll be signs up in the morning. Right now

I've got work to do." And with one last piercing look at her, he turned and disappeared back into the darkness.

Carol stared after him. If she had known how to use the bow and arrow, she might have. She wasn't used to such rudeness . . . but neither was she used to being looked at in quite that way. Her skin actually tingled.

Jet lag, she thought, rubbing her hands up and down her arms. It was a long flight in from Atlanta, and now *she* had work to do too. With a shake of her head she went off to find her new office.

At dawn the next morning Carol was back in the lobby of the Ocotillo. In daylight, it had lost its strangeness; the arrogant mystery man was gone, and the art display was nothing more than a collection of old things sitting on shelves. She barely gave it a glance. What *she* noticed was the comforting similarity between this and the lobby of the towering Atlanta property she'd just left. There was the familiar Palm-Resort ambience of a four-star, world-class hotel: The pleasing sound of water tumbling over an indoor fountain; the well-modulated tones of the front desk staff; the soft talk and laughter of guests strolling toward the dining room.

Outside, of course, there was a world of difference. Gone were the city streets, the traffic, the crush of people, and the noise. Guests arriving at the Ocotillo thought they'd traveled to the edge of the world.

And in a way they were right. It was the edge of the ordinary world, the gateway to the strange and beautiful desert world of the Southwest.

The hotel sprawled across the valley floor, the main lodge surrounded by luxurious one- and two-story adobe *casitas*, elegant suites with bedrooms, Jacuzzis, beehive fireplaces in the living rooms, and private patios. Encircling it all were the red cliffs and sandstone mesas that made Arizona famous. It was a spectacular landscape etched against a vivid, sun-drenched indigo sky.

But Carol was glad to deal with only the familiar and expected on this bright October morning. She was having trouble getting past her nervousness, a growing sense of unease that had haunted her since the night that eerie dream became yet another reason for sleeplessness. This is just new-job jitters, she assured herself. It's only the move and all. Calm down, Lawson.

What saved her was knowing that on the outside, at least, she looked perfectly calm. In a slim silk suit and a tailored blouse, her pale blond hair falling in an elegant sweep against her cheeks, she *looked like* the new assistant manager in charge of guest relations. She had worked long and hard for the promotion to that title, and she intended to use it to her best advantage. That was what life was all about, wasn't it? Careful planning that got you what you wanted . . . what you had to have. This time she would do it right. Never again would she be forced to make the kind of decision she'd made nine years earlier. She shivered.

It would be nine years on October twenty-fifth. The date was seared into her heart, a scar that wouldn't heal.

Quickly she pushed her private thoughts aside and readied a smile for the general manager's approach. "Good morning, Mr. LeGrand."

"Good morning, Ms. Lawson. I wanted to welcome you again and make certain everything is satisfactory in your department. I'm impressed that you came in last night, a commendable idea. And I also like your plan to staff the concierge desk yourself while Louise is on vacation. I think you'll find our guests are quite discriminating and can be . . . let us say, quite demanding."

"That is exactly why I enjoy working for PalmResorts. And this will give me the chance to familiarize myself with procedures and determine what changes I might like to make."

"Good. Please feel free to call me if you should run into any problems—"

"Thank you, but I'm sure there won't *be* any problems."

And then he left her alone.

"All right. Here I go," she whispered, lifting the blond, silken shock of hair off of her neck to let the air-conditioning cool her flushed skin. She slid into the chair behind the huge mahogany concierge desk. It faced the entrance to the lobby where wide glass doors framed a vista of cacti and mesas. To her right was the reception area, behind her the glass display cases. Her eyes were drawn that way, to where the shadows had hidden the dark-eyed stranger, and again she felt that unexpected tingle of excitement play across her skin. She pushed it away and got to work.

By the time the phone rang for the first time, she was ready for anything.

"Good morning. Concierge desk, may I help you? Yes, Mrs. Kern, the Jeep tours will be ready to go at nine. Your driver will meet you here at my desk. . . .

"Good morning." Another bright smile. "Yes, all the arrangements are made for your trail rides. The wrangler will pick you up out front. Look for a red van. . . .

"Good morning! Yes, I arranged for an afternoon tour of Sedona. . . .

"Good morning, Mrs. Watson. Yes, I have a driver coming to get you at exactly one-fifteen, and I reconfirmed your husband's one o'clock tee-off time. And then I have you both scheduled for the five o'clock sunset Jeep tour. . . . Yes, that can include a bottle of champagne if you would like. No problem at all. You're very welcome."

She was just catching her breath, and catching up on the paperwork and billing, when the phone rang again at ten. Dr. Marcus in suite 22 wanted a Jeep tour at eleven.

"We keep missing the morning tours at nine," he apologized. "Just can't seem to roll out of bed that early on vacation. See what you can do and get back to me, okay?"

But checking and rechecking all the company brochures didn't do a bit of good. Reluctantly she dialed suite 22. "Dr. Marcus, I'm afraid there are no tours scheduled at that time. There is an afternoon trip, with space available, at one-thirty. Can I book you and your wife on that tour?"

"That's not going to work for us. We have a three o'clock tee-off time. Can you work something out, maybe a private tour? My wife's really counting on this. Why don't you check on it and call me back, okay?"

"Of course. I'd be happy to."

After ten minutes of pleading with four different companies, she was steeling herself for Dr. Marcus's displeasure. There was only one possibility left. She dialed, and this time she got lucky.

"Great!" She smiled, straightening the pile of paper on her desk, running a polished pink nail along the edges as she talked. "Oh, I don't care if he's a regular driver or not, as long as he's good and *available*. Have him here by eleven. Tell him to ask for Lawson. Thanks."

She called the doctor with her good news, then settled back to work. She had almost cleared off her desk when a dark shadow fell across the smooth mahogany top. Before she could look up, she sensed his presence, and then there was this voice, low and husky, lifting goose bumps along her arms.

"Lonesome?"

Her head snapped up, her eyes meeting his dark, piercing gaze. He startled her, and stole her breath away. "Pardon me?" she whispered.

"I was told to ask for Lonesome. I guess that's you. I didn't think we'd be meeting again so soon."

It took Carol less than a heartbeat to realize that this tall, gorgeous man with the brash grin was the one she'd met at midnight.

He stood there, watching her in return, waiting for an answer . . . or was it a reaction? His own face, half-hidden by the brim of his Stetson, didn't give away a thing.

Keeping her voice absolutely neutral, she masked her emotions and stood, offering her hand. "My name is Lawson. Carol Lawson. And you are?"

"Cody Briggs," he answered, taking her hand. "Mesa Tours sent me."

His tone was cool, but his touch sent an unexpected heat racing along her nerves.

Carol drew her hand away but held her gaze steady. She'd have to watch herself with this man . . . which would be a lot easier if he wasn't so damn good to look at. He was incredibly handsome in a hard, sexy, dangerous way. The danger was what she felt most, a quick tightening of her stomach, an urge to run. Even as the thought crossed *her* mind, *his* muscles seemed to tense.

Carol's eyes widened. He was reading her thoughts! She could see herself mirrored in the black depths of his eyes, and it was as if he were drawing her in, closer and closer, until that dark gaze could pierce her very soul.

Carol sat back down behind the comforting wall of her desk. Picking up a pencil, she tapped it on the reservation book. "So, you're here for my special tour. Give me a minute to finish up this reservation slip and I'll fill you in on the details."

"Fill me in?" Cody laughed, annoyance roughing the sound. "Don't bother. The only thing I need to know is their names. I make up the rest as I go."

Carol bristled. "Well, that's fine as long as the guest gets what he wants——"

"Satisfaction guaranteed." Cody's dark eyes were unreadable, but there was a hint of something there, flickering like a flame in the darkness.

He hadn't meant to be so brusk, hadn't planned on it. But he hadn't planned on her either. She'd lingered at the edge of his consciousness all night and all morning. Those eyes, that face . . . he saw them in his sleep. But there was something else, something more. When their eyes met, he felt naked, raw. His body grew hard and hot. All because of one glance from a woman who was trying to tell him how to do his job.

The way he was looking at her made Carol's throat tighten in fear . . . or excitement. Neither was acceptable at the moment. Turning the pencil end over end, she surreptitiously slid her gaze up and down his tall, muscled frame. He was wearing an ankle-length canvas duster, cowboy boots, tight, worn jeans with a holster of some kind on his hip, and a red bandanna tied loosely around his neck. He looked a little too wild for the Ocotillo. And the way he stood there, thumbs hooked in his belt, arrogant, impatient——

"Want me to turn around so you can get a better look?" Cody drawled.

"Not at all." She didn't know if it was his cowboy good looks or his attitude that had her momentarily nonplussed, but neither was going to get the best of her. She could send him away. All she had to decide was whether she wanted to face a disappointed guest.

Cody rocked back on his heels. "Well?" He nodded toward the phone. "The meter's running."

With a chilly smile Carol folded her hands on her desk. "Your boss said you're not the regular guide. Have you done this before?"

Cody looked at her from under the brim of his hat as if he were actually deciding whether or not to answer. Then he shrugged; a whiplike flicker of a grin touched his lips and lit his eyes. "Yup."

Carol waited for more of an explanation, but none was forthcoming. Now, however, she was on her own turf. Crossing her long legs, she asked calmly, "Is there a route y'all follow, some normal tour with specified stops and things? I was looking at the brochures and noticed that they all go to Horseshoe Canyon, and Lost Gulch—"

Cody held out the keys. "You want to drive? No? Fine, then stop worrying. I'll give them a tour they won't forget, I promise. Just send them outside; I'll be waiting in the Jeep. And, Lonesome, anytime you want to check up on me, just book a tour."

Without another word he turned and strode out the door, duster billowing and spurs jangling. Carol stared after him for a long moment, then pushed her hair back from her face. Her nerves jumped. He might be gorgeous, but he was one arrogant son-of-a-gun. Then why did his shadow still linger on her like a touch? Why did it beckon her to follow?

Drawing a deep, steadying breath, Carol pulled herself together. Smoothing the wrinkles out of her skirt and the tremor out of her voice, she called Dr. Marcus and went on with her work.

At two forty-five the doctor tore through the front door and headed straight for Carol's desk.

Carol braced herself. All through lunch she'd regretted her decision to let Cody Briggs take her guests out. She had sensed danger; she should have taken a firmer stand. Now she was going to get chewed out for that man's incompetence—

"Ms. Lawson," the doctor said, slapping a hand onto her desk. "That was incredible. I cannot thank you enough. I mean, that was more than a tour, it was an amazing . . . no, an *enlightening* experience. Thank you for finding us such a fascinating guide."

Carol sat openmouthed for a second when he was gone, then looked across the lobby. Cody Briggs was leaning casually against the glass wall near the front entrance, his shirt unbuttoned at the neck, sleeves rolled over tanned forearms, his bandanna rolled and tied around his forehead as if he were some Indian warrior. He'd been waiting for her to look up. Now he stared back at her, one dark brow climbing slightly, an I-told-you-so grin on his face. When he touched two fingers to the brim of his hat in mock salute, Carol's blood reached a boil.

The pencil snapped in her fingers, the sound echoing like a gunshot around the quiet lobby. Heads turned. Mortified, Carol glanced down, then up again as if to place the blame squarely where it belonged, on Cody's broad shoulders. But in that instant he'd left.

TWO

"So, Lonesome, how'd I do?"

Cody's voice broke the silence of the twilit hotel garden, startling her. He wasn't certain why he'd made the special effort to be there, to speak to her, but forces that Cody respected seemed to want it to happen. All afternoon an inner voice had whispered her name, and her face had haunted him.

Now Carol's blue eyes were flashing. She hadn't seen him standing there among the long, swaying arms of the ocotillo; he seemed to materialize out of nowhere. "You frightened me."

"Yeah. I often have that effect on people," he said softly, responding to her anger. "Sorry."

She barely registered his apology, she was so busy trying not to stare at him. In jeans and a T-shirt, his bronzed skin glowing in the dusk, he looked impossibly cool and powerful, untouched by heat or dust or weariness. She felt the strangest urge to run a fingertip along the curve of muscle in his arm and down his strong forearm with its fine dark hair. Every time she was near him, her guard, which she had fine-tuned over the last nine years, seemed to crumble. It made her very nervous.

"Forget it." She shrugged, feeling her silk blouse cling to the dampness at her breasts and shoulders. "I overreacted. I'm tired and hot, that's all."

Without warning, Cody reached out and brushed a damp strand of her hair back from her face. Against his dark skin, the paleness of her hair seemed to glow like fairy light. It sifted through his fingers like the pollen of a thousand flowers. He frowned at the unexpected pleasure he was feeling, at the surge of desire that heated his loins, but he was unwilling or unable to take his hand away. Finally he mastered himself. His hand dropped to his side. "It's the desert. You'll get used to it."

The sound of his voice woke her from the trance his touch had evoked. "Of course." She laughed shakily, struggling for composure. "I know I will. There's just so much that's different here."

"Everything's different here."

Carol refused to meet his gaze. She plucked at the throat of her blouse. "Well, it certainly is a far cry from Atlanta. I was at PalmResort's high-rise property there, downtown on Peachtree." *Quiet, Lawson,* she thought. *You're starting to babble.* But she couldn't help herself. "This was a promotion. I . . . I grabbed it before I ever looked at a map to see where Carefree, Arizona, was."

"Is," he corrected with a grin. "Do you know where you are now?" Stepping so close, she could feel the heat from his body, he pointed off to the east. "Out there are the Superstition Mountains. There, the Mazatzals, then the Verde Valley, the Agua Fria . . . and then the desert. All the rest, all around, is desert." He had turned them both in a circle, his body guiding hers as if in a dance, and for just an instant Carol felt light-headed. What would it feel like to really be held in this man's arms, to move with him to some faint music, swaying, turning?

Where were these thoughts coming from? Shaking her head, Carol took a step back. "You forgot Phoenix. It's out there too, unless the pilot was lying when we touched down."

"Oh, the city." Cody dismissed it with a shrug. Then he looked down at her, a sudden playfulness in his dark gaze. "Maybe it isn't there. Maybe it's vanished and all that exists are cacti and mesquite, road-runners and javelinas, coyotes getting ready to howl at the moon."

"I thought wolves howl," Carol said softly, her face upturned to his.

"Maybe you're right. Maybe I'm making it all up." His eyes were dark and laughing. His words, his gaze were all a mystery daring to be unraveled.

If she'd been home, or even in the hotel, she'd have thought of something clever to say. Now clever-ness eluded her. It was the heat . . . the shimmer of heat in the air, the heat of his body so close in the twilight. How could mere temperature have such a strange and disquieting effect? Her thoughts were whirling.

"I've got to go," she said quickly, turning toward the low adobe building where the management employees were housed. "I'm tired and hot. I've got to get back to my room."

"I'll walk with you."

She actually quickened her step away. "No, don't. Thanks anyway." The minute the words were out, she regretted them. Or did she? That was her usual response to a guy's come-on. Why change now? Yet she turned to face him. "No, don't. But thank you anyway."

"You already said that," he replied softly.

"I know, but I didn't mean to say it so harshly."

He studied her expression with a strange intensity. "You're hard on yourself, aren't you? I wonder why."

She knew why. She always knew why. The decision she'd had to make nine years ago had taught her that lesson. If she'd been harder on herself then, more careful, more sensible, the world would be different now. Pain enveloped her. With her hands hugging her elbows, she backed away. "Good night, Mr. Briggs."

Behind her, Cody lifted a hand. He had this overwhelming need to touch her, to soothe her. But he stuffed both hands in his pockets when she turned back to face him.

"Oh, by the way, the answer to your question is yes, you did fine today. Dr. Marcus was satisfied with the tour. More than satisfied. I think he actually used the word 'enlightening.'" She finished with a rough little laugh that held no happiness.

That little sound made Cody want to pull her into his arms and comfort her, protect her. He could sense the pain she was struggling with, the sadness that shadowed her eyes, her face, her smile. It tore at his heart. She called up feelings from his soul that surprised and unnerved him. He thought he had pushed all that away, too angry to do anything but work and curse, yet every time he got within a mile of her, there came this flood of emotion. Like a flash flood in the desert, it would probably leave chaos in its wake.

"I'd take that with a grain of salt." He shrugged coolly.

"Believe me, I did." But he'd made her smile. Steering the conversation onto safer ground, Carol lifted one pale brow. "So, I guess the real reason you came back this evening was to brag."

Cody pushed his hat back on his head and grinned at her. "As the saying goes, 'It's not bragging if you can do it.'" The laugh lines around his eyes and mouth softened the sharp planes and angles of his face, making him even more handsome and somehow younger, more boyish, like a young Clint Eastwood.

Carol rolled her eyes heavenward, seeking relief. This cowboy stuff was just too much. Yet she had to admit there was something irresistible in the broad grin and those glinting dark eyes. Cowboy grin, Indian eyes . . . broad shoulders and lean hips, spurs that jingle . . . jangle . . . jingle. No wonder they called it the wild West. A flicker of a smile danced in her cool blue eyes, warming them to sapphire. "The doctor must be an easy touch."

Cody laughed. "Must be. But not you, huh?"

Carol shook her head, making her blond hair swing in an arc around her face. "Not me. I'm a tough customer."

"Are you?" He looked at her, somehow seeing right through to the secret place in her soul . . . seeing the truth.

Carol felt the power of his gaze and turned away. "You bet I am. And now I'm going in. It's been a long day."

"It's going to be a beautiful sunset," he mused, looking off toward the mesas edging the horizon. "If you've never seen an Arizona sunset, you should pull out a chair, put up your feet, and watch the sky. It can be amazing—"

"Thank you, but I have other plans."

"Good. So do I. It wasn't an invitation, only a suggestion." The teasing in his smile took the sting out of his words.

Still, Carol felt torn by conflicting emotions. Trouble was, she was too darn tired to figure it all out. "Good night."

He touched two fingers to the brim of his hat, a typical Cody farewell. "Good evening, Lonesome."

He watched her walk away, her slender body moving beautifully under her clothes, her pale hair glimmering in the light. She was like a sip of cool water in the desert, this blond, lovely woman . . . and he suddenly was a very thirsty man. But there was something else, something he'd seen in her eyes that drew him yet pushed him away at the same time. She wasn't what she appeared, any more than he was.

Now, eyes narrowed as he strode out into the sun, he headed for his rendezvous with the desert.

Alone in her room, Carol sank onto the couch. She had stripped off her clothes and left them in a pile on the floor. Tilting back her head, she felt the air-conditioning flow over her skin, stilling the fevered rush of her thoughts and the unwelcome prickle of emotion that Cody had aroused.

Oh, just the thought of him brought the heat rushing back again, deep down inside where cool air was no help at all. It was like a small flame burning there at the core of her body, something that felt oddly, remarkably, like desire.

But that was impossible. She had a life, friends, a whole raft of plans that didn't include any brash, dark-eyed stranger. Yet she couldn't stop thinking about him. And she couldn't sit still!

Needing to do *something*, she gathered her clothes and put them in the hamper, ran the tub, filled it to overflowing with bubbles, and finally climbed in. Tucking a towel behind her neck, she leaned back and closed her eyes.

Back home it was already eight o'clock. Back home she used to put on shorts and a T-shirt and jog the three miles down Peachtree to Matthew's condo. *Matthew*, she mused. After two years of dating, it had been surprisingly simple to end the relationship. She'd blamed distance, but the truth was, there'd been no passion, no excitement, no fire burning in her veins. Even without the move to Arizona, that was destined to end. But she could have grabbed her friend Jill after work and the two of them would have gone to Houston's and sat out on the patio and sipped margueritas. It sounded awfully good right now . . . fun, familiar.

Carol let out a little sigh that stirred the bubbles. See, that's all she was feeling: A bad case of homesickness. That explained the yearning, the strange disquiet. No wonder she felt so jumpy, so utterly vulnerable.

Are you sure? a little voice whispered in her head. *All those years back home you were waiting, hoping, dreaming of something to fill the emptiness in your heart. And Atlanta didn't do it, not work, not friends, nothing has filled that void. It will have to be something wonderful, something magical . . . something waiting out there in a secret place and time. That's what has you yearning, aching, dreaming you can fly. . . .*

"What?" She gasped, sitting up so quickly, the water sloshed onto the floor and soaked the bath mat. Had she drifted off into another of those strange dreams?

"Darn," she muttered. "Darn, darn, darn! What a mess." Stepping out of the tub, she carefully mopped up the floor with the bath mat, toweled off, then pulled on a robe with the PalmResort logo stitched on the breast pocket, and tied it around her waist. She took a cold Corona out of the tiny fridge that came with the room and sipped at it while she opened a little cellophane-wrapped package of crackers. In a week or two she'd find an apartment of her own in Phoenix, which existed whether Cody Briggs thought so or not.

Him. He was impossible to forget, and that's what disturbed her. As if they had a will of their own, her thoughts fastened on to the image of that Indian-eyed, hard-bodied man. And with the image came that flicker of heat deep in her body.

Well, the tub hadn't worked. And sleep was hours off. Maybe a nice picturesque sunset would be soothing after all.

She flopped down on a chaise on the patio. It was quiet there, shaded, screened for privacy by a row of flowering shrubs. But her view was incredible. And, though she was glad she didn't have to admit it face-to-face, he had been right: It *was* a beautiful sunset. The sky was tinged pink and peach, with gold-dipped clouds sailing near the horizon. And just below them, the mesas sailed like huge stone ships, their prows pointing to the distance. Pointing to the unknown, the unexplored, the undiscovered. Dark red in daytime, now the mesas caught the last rays of the sun on their tops and were burnished gold and orange. Their carved sides held shadows and secrets in dark folds and crevices. Even the sand at their base was golden, so lovely and quiet, dotted with the soft shapes of the sagebrush.

Carol leaned back, eyes half-closed, and took a sip

of her beer. Then something appeared, there at the very top of the mesa, etched against the orange sky. It seemed to be a figure running, a *man* running with his chest and legs bare and his long, dark hair flying behind him. He moved from light to darkness, from man to silhouette, from real to imagined, and then he disappeared.

She straightened up with a start. Her eyes were wide, and her body tingled with fright. "I know this. I've seen it before. But how?" It didn't take her two seconds to remember her dream: The running man, the eagle, the old Indian. But now she was wide-awake. This shouldn't be happening.

She rubbed a hand over her eyes. "I don't understand. How could I have dreamed about something that didn't happen until now? How could I have dreamed about a place I've never seen before? What is going on?"

But there was no one to answer her.

Except Jill. Friends as well as coworkers at Palm-Resorts, she could talk to Jill about almost anything.

She hurried inside and dialed, then snuggled onto the couch, legs tucked beneath her, counting the rings. "Come on, buddy, be there, plea—Jill? Hi, it's me!"

"Carol? What a treat."

Her voice sounded so wonderfully warm and familiar, it made the tears rise to Carol's eyes. "Oh, for me too. It's so good to talk to you, Jill. I miss y'all. It's hot out here and so different—"

"Different's good, remember? It's what you wanted."

"But this is *so* different. Weird. And weird things are happening to me."

"What? The job? Your boss?"

"No, *he's* not the problem."

There was a tiny pause. "Oh? Did I hear a strange emphasis on that 'he'? If not him, then who?"

Carol could almost see Jill's brows climb in eager anticipation. She shifted the phone to her other ear and tightened the sash on her robe. "No one. Well . . . there is this man—"

"Really? Tell me about him."

"No, it's nothing. That's not why I called—"

"Darn. For just a second there I thought maybe you'd finally let go of the past and begun living in the present." There was a moment of silence, an emptiness on the line. Then Jill said softly, "There, I've done it again, haven't I? Pushed too hard. Now I've ruined our phone call. I'm sorry, Carol. Honest. I miss you already, and I only want you to be happy."

"I know. I'm not angry. I'm really just confused."

"Okay, so tell me, who is this man?"

"He . . . he's a Jeep driver for a tour company. His name is Cody Briggs."

"Cody Briggs! Spurs? Chaps? A great cowboy butt in tight worn jeans?"

"All that and more. But really, he is not the problem. He's just sort of a mystery. But that's not what's worrying me."

"Then what is? Tell Doctor Jill."

"You won't think I'm crazy?"

"I'd love you anyway. That's what friends are for."

Carol smiled. "Okay. Well, do you remember the dream I told you about? The strange one I had the night before I left Atlanta?"

"I think so. Why?"

"Well, I keep having it. Sort of. Parts of it. But . . . when I'm awake."

"Stop. Wait. *Now* you're scaring me. What do you mean, 'when you're awake'?"

"Well, most of the time it's just a feeling, like there's something there waiting just beyond the range of my vision . . . something about to happen. And then this evening I was sitting out on the patio, and there was a man running, just like in the dream."

"A man running . . . ?" Jill's voice relaxed. "Heck, Carol, if I went and looked out the window, I could probably see a dozen men running. Of course, some of them make you wonder why they think they look good in spandex, but jogging's the in thing, remember?"

"Jill, this is not Atlanta, and this man wasn't jogging. He was running bare-chested across the top of a mesa."

"And how did *he* look?"

"Jill!"

"Well, that's important. If you're going to start seeing things, they may as well be great to look at."

Carol laughed, feeling the comfort of Jill's irreverent humor. "Yes, Jill, he was far away . . . but fabulous."

"Good. Then I'm not the least bit worried. Hey, you were a wreck before you left, between the move and breaking up with Matthew, and now you're in a strange place with a new job . . . and knowing you, you're already working too hard. PalmResorts doesn't give medals, remember. They barely give raises."

"But they do give promotions," Carol countered.

"Yes, so enjoy yours. Eat some Häagen-Dazs ice cream, get some sleep, and relax. Okay?"

"Okay." Carol nodded, smiling as if Jill were right there, red hair springing around her freckled face. "And thanks for the pep talk. I miss you. I'll call again soon."

"Me too. Hugs. Bye."

Putting the phone down, Carol drew a deep breath. There, everything was fine, normal, just the way it should be.

THREE

With a full hotel, Carol needed every wrangler, hot-air-balloon-tour *and* Jeep-tour guide available. Yet she avoided using Cody Briggs whenever possible.

It didn't seem to make sense, because when he did take out a tour the guests came back singing his praises. A man stopped at her desk to exclaim: "That was incredible. I didn't know you could *eat* parts of desert plants!" A woman returned from an afternoon tour, rested her Gucci bag on the desk and murmured, "I have never heard anyone *chant* like that. It was thrilling."

Carol smiled stiffly. There it was: That sense of danger. Again she crossed his name off the list for the next morning.

But a full moon meant the sunset tours were swamped. Just a day later she found herself reluctantly penciling in his name, seeing in her mind Cody's lean, hard body, his dark, unreadable eyes, sensing immediately that unexpected surge of heat that felt strangely like desire. Annoyed with herself, she pushed the vision away. One more tour would surely be all right. What could possibly happen?

She purposefully stayed at the desk past nine, until that last tour was safely in. Carol closed her ledger and pushed back her chair when the honeymoon couple she had sent out with Cody strolled into the lobby. The husband made a beeline to her desk. "Hi, Ms. Lawson. Didn't expect you to be here so late, but it gives me a chance to thank you. That was absolutely amazing. The scenery was great, but it was that guide! He's . . . well, he's inspiring. Did you know tarantulas can walk on your hand? And you can hypnotize a rattlesnake . . . or at least, *he* can!"

That did it. *She* was not about to be hypnotized by that mysterious, dark-eyed man. She'd been sending guests on tours without knowing what was really going on out there, but no more. The hotel had certain liabilities and she, as assistant manager, had certain clearly defined responsibilities. One of those was *not* to send her guests out into possible danger.

Her skin prickled with the thought. No wonder she felt so strange when he was around, as if she could sense his presence before she ever caught a glimpse of him. No wonder his image lingered behind her eyes. He could be dangerous. The only logical thing to do was take the tour herself on her first day off.

A day in the desert with Cody Briggs. . . . She could almost feel the heat, or was that the startling warmth of excitement and anticipation? Neither, she assured herself. This was strictly business. But the thought of being alone with him tantalized her, playing at the edge of her consciousness even while she willed herself back to work.

She was in the middle of apologizing to yet another guest for the unavailability of tours on Saturday morning when Cody strode into the lobby, his boots sounding like war drums on the polished wood floor.

"Have we got a problem?" he demanded, his voice a low growl. He rested both hands on Carol's desk and leaned toward her. This woman was trying to tell him how to do his job. Beautiful as she was, that was not going to happen.

Carol scooted her chair back and held up one hand, trying to finish her phone call. "I am really sorry, Mr. Shafer, but all the tours are booked for today. Could I possibly . . . no," she lowered her voice, swinging her chair around so her back was to Cody, "No, I'm afraid he is not available. Yes, so I've been told, but I'm afraid he is not available today. No, not tomorrow either, but I will try to find—Yes, I'll call you back."

Drawing a deep, steadying breath, she turned her chair around and hung up the phone.

"Hello, Cody. Can I help you?"

"What the hell is going on here?"

"Pardon me?"

"You heard me." He drew himself to his full height, all six feet two inches of sinew and muscle, and glared off across the lobby, trying to rein in his temper. The brim of his hat cast a shadow across his eyes, but there was no missing the hard line of his mouth, the cut of his jaw. He looked fierce, and for just a second Carol thought she had good reason to be afraid of him. Her heart tightened in alarm, and a shudder of fear swept through her.

"Cody, let me explain—"

"I don't want explanations, and I won't have you telling me how to do my job!" He pinned her to her chair with a savage, relentless gaze. The recent past came roaring at him with all its bitterness and betrayal. He barely saw the woman who sat there braving his rage.

The phone rang, but Cody's hand was quicker. "Concierge desk. Please call back in ten minutes." He hung up, then set the receiver aside. "You've got to deal with me first, Lonesome."

Grace under fire was an old Southern tradition. Leaning back in her chair, Carol stared straight back at him. "If y'all are willing to hear me out now, I'll be happy to explain my decisions."

"You mean you actually have an explanation for what you're doing?" Cody's dark eyes searched her face, and slowly the black irises warmed, gold flecks appearing like sparks dancing on smoldering coals. "Okay, go ahead and explain. And it better be good, because I want this work. I need to do this."

"I'm sure you do. But I need to be sure of *how* you do it before I can continue to employ you."

That was the threat he'd been expecting. *Continue*

to employ me? he thought. He'd sure as hell heard those words before. Those words ticked him off. But this time he held his temper, gritting his teeth.

"Careful, aren't you?" he said, his gaze as penetrating as a searchlight.

She nodded, returning look for look. "Yes. It saves a lot of grief later on."

"Do you really think you can always be careful enough? On guard against all the possibilities in the universe?" he scoffed.

"Maybe not. But you can try."

Having said more than she'd intended, Carol looked away. Until now she'd felt as if he were trying to see into her soul, but had he? Could he? Shaking her head, she swiveled the chair so that he had only her profile to stare at so intently. She pointed off into the bright sunlight glaring outside the door.

"I want to know exactly what y'all do out there with my guests."

"I give them a tour." He shrugged, sliding his hands into the pockets of his jeans. "I show them the desert. I tell them stories—"

"See!" Carol interrupted. "That's exactly what I mean. You're not supposed to be telling them stories. You're supposed to point out some interesting landmarks, fill in a little history, give them a few facts to write home about on postcards."

"I see. So they've complained?"

"No, they haven't, but—"

"What *have* they said?" Cody leaned forward again, his dark eyes shining with confidence. It was a heady combination, that brashness paired with his powerful physical presence. No wonder he could hypnotize snakes. Carol tried to look away.

"What *do* the guests say? Tell me," he demanded.

She felt the ground slip away. "They . . . they say your tours are interesting."

"Interesting?" he repeated, one dark brow lifting. He had his hair tied back today, so that she saw clearly the swoop of that dark brow above his black eyes, the sharp curve of his cheekbones, the sensuality of his beautiful, chiseled mouth.

She drew her shoulders back slightly. "They say you do strange things."

The corner of his lips twitched, amusement lighting his whole face. "Define strange," he challenged.

"I would call chanting strange. And eating desert plants. And hypnotizing snakes—"

"Hypnotizing snakes?" He grinned.

"That's what I've heard," she answered, fighting back a smile. He *was* outrageous, but gorgeous too. And somehow irresistible.

"What?" he demanded. "Right then, what were you thinking?"

"Nothing," she said quickly. "That is none of your business."

"It is if it's what's really motivating you."

He knew at that moment that she was vulnerable, and he could force an answer from her, but that very vulnerability touched him. He'd back off for now. He'd wait. Instead he said very calmly, "There's nothing strange in what I do, Carol. I know the desert. I celebrate its beauty, I use its power. I'm the best guide you'll ever find. Let me take out the tours. It's important to me."

"Surely you could find another job."

"I want this one," he replied.

Sure, there were other things he could be doing, *should* be doing. The research on his next book, for example. Or verifying the authenticity of the two dozen artifacts sitting on his shelves back home. But neither of those would keep him in front of an audience eager to learn about the desert he loved, *nor* close to this blue-eyed woman with the little worried frown creasing her brow. Unexplainably, those were the only two things that suddenly seemed to matter.

It was his turn to frown. What he really wanted to do was draw a fingertip across those pale brows and erase the crease that lingered there far too often. He wanted to understand what worried her, and smooth that away too. Her lovely eyes should shine with happiness, and he'd like to put it there, then hang around to feel her soft gaze caress his face. To tell the truth, since the minute he'd first met her, he'd been yearning to feel the caress of more than just her eyes.

Cody tore *his* gaze away, squinting off into the safe, bright sunlight. *Get a grip, Briggs!* he growled silently. *Focus on the present. You came here with a purpose. Stick to that.*

"So, do I get my job back?"

Carol set both hands flat on her desk. "Perhaps. With one condition—"

"What?" he said, already on guard. "I can't give

you a detailed itinerary; the desert changes daily, and if it's worth anything, the tour has to also. And I won't rattle off some prepackaged drivel. There's magic out there; it's worth talking about. So what else? What is it? My appearance? Is that what makes you nervous? 'Cause that I *can* change."

He shrugged the duster off and dropped it on her desk, its dusty folds burying her ledger. "Enough? Or is it the hat? The neckerchief?" He tossed each on the center of her desk, a mocking glint sharp in his eyes. "Or maybe it's the shirt? The belt? The—"

"Stop! Don't!" Carol cried out, her eyes following the path of his hands down his body. Unable to help herself, her gaze touched for just a second on the fly of his jeans. The tight, faded denim that outlined his lean hips and muscular thighs also revealed the bulge of his sex. Desire flickered through her, fast and hot.

Standing so that her eyes were level with his face instead of his crotch, Carol glared at him. "Don't you dare make a scene here on my territory."

Cody shook his head, his mood shifting like quicksilver. "I wouldn't. It was just a joke," he said simply. He picked up his duster, settled his hat back on his head. "Sorry. I know how it feels to take a job so seriously it hurts." He started to walk away.

"Cody, you never let me finish," Carol said, the softness of her voice turning him around. "The condition was that you take me out on a tour on Monday, my day off. Deal?"

A slow grin spread across his face. "Deal. And to

prove I'm a good guy, we'll make it a private tour. Free. I'll pick you up at nine."

"Ten. I've got to get some sleep."

"Fine. And, Lonesome . . . wear jeans." With a tip of his hat he strode off.

Carol stared after him, her chest rising and falling with rapid, shallow breaths. Somehow he seemed to have taken all the air with him when he left. She shook her head, wondering what she was getting into. She was scared *and* excited, two emotions that didn't seem to go together but somehow combined in the presence of Cody Briggs into a dizzying anticipation.

Sliding into her chair, she opened the ledger, flipped to Monday, and next to Cody's name, penciled in one word: Me.

FOUR

Monday dawned bright and clear. Carol knew because she lay there watching the stars fade and the sky lighten to robin's-egg-blue. Her emotions were far less tranquil. Her stomach was tied in knots, her heart racing, and all because she was going to spend the day with Cody Briggs.

It was crazy. She had left Atlanta, family, and friends with less trepidation than she felt this morning. It was *his* fault! Cody attracted her, confused her, unnerved her all at the same time, leaving her filled with emotions she didn't want and couldn't handle. What was it about him? His dark, searching eyes? His hard body? His boldness? No. There was something else that was the sum of all that powerful physical appeal yet more, some unexplainable connection between them.

Her feet hit the floor. That was nonsense. No one could touch her heart if she didn't want him to. She knew that, she'd proved it, and all her fear was nothing but old ghosts rattling at a closet door. But it was locked. She was safe. All she had to do was be careful not to let him cross the line.

Besides, she was probably imagining it all. Their relationship—which wasn't a relationship at all, she assured herself—was strictly business, hindered by distrust and misunderstanding. Today was simply a chance to set things straight and establish some clear working dynamics. Now *that* was a sensible response to Cody Briggs.

Eyes sparkling, Carol got out of bed, showered, and pulled on a pair of khaki hiking shorts and a T-shirt. She was darned if she'd wear jeans; she'd dress in a snowsuit first. However, she did hurry through the lobby ten minutes early.

Cody was already waiting out front. He had on a black T-shirt that stretched across the muscles of his chest and shoulders, worn black jeans that drew her eyes like a magnet, but no hat. Instead, his bandanna was tied around his brow, his dark hair hanging straight to his shoulders, as blue-black as a raven's wing.

"Oh!" There it was again, that irrational urge to push her fingers through that wild, dark hair, to feel the strong line of his jaw, the roll of muscle along his shoulders, his forearms. She wanted to touch him, taste him. . . . The realization stunned her. Hadn't she just warned herself about the danger? Where had her self-control flown to?

To cover her discomfort she slowed her step, lifting her pale brows quizzically.

"What? No duster, Mr. Briggs?"

"No jeans, Miss Lawson?" he drawled with an answering grin.

As intently as she'd been studying him, so had he been watching her. There was something about this woman, something he couldn't explain which drew him to her as if there'd never been another woman in the world. It was as if he knew her, as if he'd been waiting for her.

And he had been waiting, parked there in the big circular drive in everyone's way, for forty-five minutes, anticipating her arrival. That didn't make any sense and he knew it, but he'd thought about her from dusk through dawn and couldn't wait another minute. Now she was walking closer with that sweet sway of her hips, her pale hair swinging, her eyes as blue as the morning sky . . . wearing shorts. Why had he expected anything else?

His brash grin made Carol feel all prickly. She tipped up her chin. "You're parked right in everyone's way, Cody. You should have parked around the back."

He laughed, a rich, husky sound without a hint of contrition, as if he'd known exactly what she was going to say. The thought made her knees go weak. She mustn't let that happen.

But it was too late. Already her pulse was racing. She licked her dry lips. "Well? Should we get this show on the road?"

"Whatever you say. Hop in." His fingers tightened around hers as he gave her a hand up onto the seat. The touch sent a jolt of awareness running up his arm and through his chest. As if he hadn't already *been* aware of every inch of her, every ripe curve of her body. Those little hiking shorts didn't help. One glance at that sassy, khaki-clad bottom as she climbed into the Jeep, and hiking was swept clear out of his thoughts. Instead he was imagining a hot embrace with hungry, eager mouths and roaming hands. With an inner groan, he dragged a tongue that felt dry as sandpaper across equally dry lips, and slammed the door shut.

All he said was, "Buckle up!" then jammed the Jeep into gear and aimed for the nearest mesa. They raced across the valley floor in silence, whizzing past sagebrush, cacti, and piles of boulders. Then abruptly they started to climb. The road, if one could call it that, was a thin line scratched along the sheer wall of the mesa. It zigzagged back and forth, climbing steadily, turning back on itself in hairpin turns.

Carol had one hand on the dashboard, one clenched around the rollbar over her head. "What happens if someone comes the other way?" she asked, finally breaking the silence.

"No problem. We just pull over to the edge and let him pass."

"The edge?" she repeated, looking straight down. "I think we're over the edge now."

"Then lets hope no one comes the other way."

She glared at him. "Is this the same way you take the guests, or are you doing this on purpose?"

"Everything I do is on purpose," he said coolly, then flicked an appraising glance her way. "And you're the same. We're alike, you and I."

"Oh no," Carol shook her head, denying it with a thin-lipped smile. "You are so wrong. I may do things on purpose, but I do them carefully. For example, if I was taking *my* boss on a tour, I'd pick the safest, sanest route . . . not go bouncing up some hill and making that person wish they were anywhere else but here."

"It's a mesa, not a hill," Cody corrected, guiding the Jeep around the last curve and up onto the flat top of the mesa where he cut the engine. "And it was perfectly safe; I make this drive every day. *And*, Carol, I don't think of you as my boss," he added, cocking one elbow on the back of his seat and shifting a lean, hard hip so that he faced her. "I'm done with bosses. Bosses and policy decisions and colleagues and all the rest of it. I prefer to think of you as a woman who may be able to make use of some of my talents. *And*—" he placed one finger on her lips, staying her attempted interruption. "And stop being angry with me, take a look around, and *then* tell me if you really wish you were somewhere else."

Carol pressed a fingertip to the still-tingling spot on her lip where he'd touched her. "Ohmygoodness," she said as her eyes swept across the landscape. All around them were row upon row of red-and-gold sandstone cliffs and mesas, rolling on endlessly toward the horizon. In between lay wide valleys dotted with saguaro and sage, juniper and piñon pine, then the shadow lines of more mesas . . . a vast, empty, hyp-notizing sight.

For Carol, used to highways and shopping centers and skyscrapers, the emptiness seemed unbelievable. Was there this much land, this much space, in all the world? Where were the people? It was as if everyone else had disappeared, and the world was an earlier place, brand-new, untouched, unchanged.

"You like it," Cody said, his voice husky with sat-isfaction.

"I've never seen anything like it," Carol whis-pered. "It's not at all what I imagined. I thought the desert was sand, like a beach or something. It's a wil-derness."

"A wildness." His love of the place was clear in his voice. "It has a great beauty and magic all its own."

"Magic?" She looked at him, too startled to scoff.

"Yes. It transforms things . . . people. You'll see."

Looking into his dark, hypnotic eyes, she believed him. Worse, she wanted to believe him. Could some magic overcome the past? Guarantee the future? Would she ever have a heart again that didn't ache and shy away from every hint of happiness? Could magic heal the hurt of having held her baby for a moment—then never again?

"What is it?" Cody asked, seing her face grow so pale and tight. "What is it, Lonesome? What did I say?"

"Why do you call me that?" Carol cried, scooting back to the door of the Jeep. She folded her arms under her breasts and glared out into the distance, fighting the tears that pooled in her eyes. "Don't call me that."

"All right," Cody said gently, wishing he could pull her against his chest, press his lips to her hair, take away her sadness. "It's all right." His voice was incredibly tender and gentle. "I didn't mean any harm, Carol. Or any insult. It was just a joke that first time, but then somehow when I looked into your eyes, I felt something . . . or I *thought* I did . . . as if there was a hurt locked deep inside you. I . . . I felt oddly connected to you. The name just stuck in my head." He shrugged, giving up on trying to explain the unexplainable and looked away to give them both some distance. "I apologize."

Carol eyed him warily, disarmed by his honesty and openness, and stunned that this arrogant dark-eyed stranger should be the first man in her life to show such sensitivity. She couldn't even think straight. All she wanted was an end to the confrontation.

"Forget it." She shrugged, waving a hand in the space between them. "It's okay. It really had nothing to do with you. I shouldn't have lost my temper."

"No, it was my fault. Sorry. I stepped over the line."

Carol jumped. Her gaze was drawn to his face. And in that instant she knew why he frightened her. He *could* see into her heart.

She covered her face with her hands.

"Oh, don't," Cody said with a groan, taking her shoulders in his big hands. "Don't cry—"

"I am *not* crying!" she snapped, glaring up at him. "Do I look like someone who's crying? I am angry, annoyed. Why do you have to keep saying these strange things? No one wants to hear them! It's exactly what I said the other day: Stick to a tour. A few landmarks, the names of a couple of cacti, a mesa here, a mountain there. Names, facts, that's all. That's all anyone wants. A *tour*, dammit. Can't you do that simple thing?"

He dropped his hands and a slow cold smile curved his lips. "Yeah. I can do that."

Twisting in his seat, Cody reached into the back and grabbed a hat. "Here. Put this on. You're so fair, the sun will fry you to a crisp. Have you got any sunscreen?"

"I'm fine. I'm in the good southern sun plenty at home. Don't y'all worry about me."

"Okay, have it your way."

"Glad we got that straight," Carol muttered, but her heart was pounding and pounding. It was this sun, the heat shimmering all around. "Here, give me that hat and let's get on with the tour. I signed up for a three-hour tour, and you must have *something* to show me besides the top of this one mesa."

"Sure. Whatever you say." With a tug on his hat brim, Cody threw the Jeep into gear and off they drove.

Coming down the sloped side of the mesa, crossing the valley floor, the Jeep bounced and bumped over stones and ruts in the road. It was all red sandstone, dry and dusty now but carrying the deeply etched scars of sudden desert rain. The silence was deafening.

Finally, Cody offered an abbreviated tour as he drove. "Enchanted Mesa. Snoring Man Mesa. Apache Peak there in the distance. The short trees are *prosopis velutina*, honey mesquite, and the Indians ground the long curved pods into flour; the Pimas made a kind of liquor out of it. The other small trees along the arroyos are *paloverde*, 'green stick,' also called Blue Paloverde, which doesn't seem to make a whole lot of sense . . . but what does?" His sideways glance flicked across her face like a touch.

Carol felt the blood climb to her cheeks.

He pulled the Jeep to a stop and jumped out. "Come on," he ordered, heading for a cluster of boulders about fifty yards away with Carol following closely behind. It was infuriating. Cody strode along with the sun on his broad shoulders and back, his long shadow gliding ahead of him, while every step gave Carol trouble. Rocks shifted under her feet, thorns scratched at her ankles, *something* slid out from behind a plant and skittered across the toe of her sneaker. "Help," she yelped, stopping in her tracks. "Something attacked me!"

"Probably an angry tour guide," Cody said with a growl. But he held out his hand. "Here, stay close and hang on to me. Nothing out here will hurt you."

"Sure! You expect me to believe you? I may be a city girl, but I've heard of rattlesnakes. I wasn't born yesterday." But despite her sarcasm, she felt herself relax.

Cody slid his fingers between hers and tightened his hold. "Come on. Compared to your Atlanta highways, you're in very little danger here."

With her hand in his, Carol now felt unexpectedly brave. She started to notice things: All the different kinds of cacti, the quick little lizards darting back and forth, the big-eared leap of a jackrabbit just ten feet away, the swoop of a bird across the bright blue sky. The air smelled of sunlight and sage, a hot spicy scent that filled her head and chest with a sweet warmth. How long had it been since she smelled real air, unpolluted, unairconditioned? It was delicious!

"Saguaro," Cody announced, standing her next to a tall, fabulously shaped cactus whose arms reached for the sky. "*Carnegiea gigantea.* This one's probably a hundred and fifty years old, fifty feet tall, and twelve tons in weight. It can live for two hundred years and survive almost anything but man's carelessness."

Carol looked from him to the saguaro, tipping her head way back to stare at the pleated, thorny trunk and the uplifted arms.

"See that?" Cody asked, pointing.

There was a hole in the trunk and a bird nested inside, one dark little eye staring back at them. "It's a white-winged dove, but cactus wrens, elf owls, and flickers all nest in saguaro. They also nest in cholla, but that's one cactus I'd stay away from with those long, bare legs of yours." He let loose a wicked grin. "Didn't trust me on the jeans idea, did you?"

She started to object, but merely shook her head and let it slide. She was feeling too mellow to argue. The heat was not at all as she'd imagined, nothing like the thick, humid heat of an Atlanta summer. Instead the sunshine and warmth seemed to shimmer, a golden lambent light that changed the look of things and made her feel disoriented, even pleasantly sleepy. And connected to all these sensations was the coolness of his hand. His grip was strong and steady, his skin smooth, though she could feel the calluses on his fingertips and palm. Strong hands, yet gentle . . . she wondered what it would be like to be caressed by this man, to feel his touch on her face, her breasts—

She shuddered, awash with desire.

"What's the matter?" he asked, though the amusement glinting in his dark eyes gave every indication that he knew all too well what she'd been thinking.

He was, the *thought* was . . . *both* were equally impossible. "Absolutely nothing. What could be wrong?"

"Nothing, as far as I'm concerned. But every time we touch you shy away like a startled deer. I'm no wolf, no panther or eagle . . . nothing to be afraid of." He was teasing now, and the combination of arrogance and humor was strangely seductive.

Carol armed herself against it. "I am anything but frightened, Cody, trust me."

"Okay," he nodded, his eyes darkening as he stepped closer. "I will, if you'll trust me."

She stood right under his chin, looking up at him,

and suddenly all she wanted was to have this man kiss her. She wanted to feel his mouth burning hers, his arms crushing her to his chest. She wanted to feel every inch of him pressed against her, from breast to belly. She wanted . . . she wanted . . .

"What?" he whispered, his breath stirring the hair at her temples. "When you look at me like that I can't think straight, Lonesome. I feel as if you're reaching for me, but pushing hard away at the same time. Are you?"

"Me?" She gasped, as if the thought were outrageous. "This heat must be getting to you, Cody. Maybe you should go lie down in the shade."

"Only if you'll join me."

Carol gave a shaky little laugh and tossed her head. "When hell freezes over."

He saw right through her. "I'm right, aren't I?" he said, narrowing his eyes. His gaze was like a laser piercing through wall after carefully constructed wall. He reached out and touched her cheek, then slid his hand into the pale silken spill of her hair, his fingers grazing her scalp.

Shivers of delight raced up and down her spine. Her eyelids fluttered. "You're wrong," she insisted. "Way off base. You don't know a thing about me."

"Let's fix that. Right now," he whispered, his breath warm on her lips.

She swayed toward him slightly, even as warning lights flashed behind her eyes. Danger. Danger. He was supposed to back off, to stay on his side of the line . . . but instead she felt them both sliding toward the edge.

She broke away, afraid now, afraid of what she was feeling. Without thinking she spun and rushed toward the Jeep, glancing behind just to make sure he was still where she'd left him.

"Ow!" she yelped, and grabbed at her right hand. Her fingers burned like fire, and when she looked she saw a fringe of needlelike white thorns stuck there.

He was at her side in a second. "Okay. No problem. Here, we'll do this the old Indian way—" and before she could react, he took her hand and rubbed it through his hair, and all the thorns fell out. Just like that.

She stood looking up at him, her hand still held between his, feeling the warm, thick brush of his ebony hair against her fingertips, a strangely sensuous and intimate sensation.

Cody looked down at her, into those cornflower-blue eyes so wary and vulnerable, and felt his heart twist in his chest. Damn! This wasn't supposed to be happening. Somewhere in the last few minutes he'd lost control—of the tour *and* his emotions. What was it about this woman? Was she stirred by the same feeling of excitement that consumed him?

Catching hold of her arms, he pulled her close against his body. She was a small, bright flame licking up his flesh from knees to chin, kindling every inch of him in between. He didn't stop to think, he acted.

His kiss was like nothing Carol had ever felt before. His mouth was firm and warm, moving over hers gently but hungrily. The touch of his lips to hers sent ripples racing across her skin. He kissed the right corner of her mouth, then the left, then drew his tongue along the full fleshy pout of her lower lip.

When she groaned, melting against him, her lips parted and he slid his tongue into the honeyed sweetness of her mouth. Her tongue met his, the tips touching and the delicious shock of that contact made them cling to each other, his arms wrapping tight around her waist, hers circling his neck. For the moment their hands were still; the kiss was everything.

Beneath Carol's feet, the world had fallen away. There was only the sweet burning heat of his kiss that was setting her heart on fire. She parted her lips again, needing to draw his sweet breath deep into her lungs, her soul. A sigh escaped her lips, an involuntary sound that was half pleasure, half pain.

A matching groan escaped Cody's throat. He slipped his hands down to the small of her back, then lower, cupping her buttocks and pulling her hips up against the fierce ache in his groin. He was burning, hot and hard with desire. His fingers kneaded her soft, sweet flesh, feeling her muscles tighten as she lifted onto tiptoe to push herself against him.

Abruptly Carol pulled away, staggering back a step to open a space between them. "I . . . I don't know how that happened," she said with a gasp, swallowing hard.

Cody's breathing was ragged, his voice husky with lust. "Neither do I, Lonesome, but it certainly felt good."

She gave a breathless laugh. "And foolish. It should never have happened. I'm sorry—"

"I'm not." His dark eyes devoured her face. "I probably will be, but not yet."

Carol quickly turned away, hurrying toward the safety of the Jeep. "Come on. I want the rest of my tour. Time's a'wasting."

He stood motionless, watching her hurry away from him, and he suddenly felt like an animal, a wild creature of the desert, surging with the instinct to hunt, to catch, to mate. He wanted this woman, dammit, like he'd never wanted anything before.

"Cody? Didn't you hear me? I want to get going." She caught hold of her elbows with her hands, arms crossed over her knotted stomach. "Why are you looking at me that way?"

"What way?"

Like a predator, she wanted to say, every sense alert to the danger and attraction. She had to swallow around the sudden tightness in her throat. "Cody, just a tour, remember? You agreed."

"So I did," he said, raking a hand through the dark mane of his hair. "All right. I'm coming."

Carol carefully kept a few steps ahead of him, but she did glance back over her shoulder, needing to lighten the tone, to disarm the power of the past few moments. "I certainly hope you don't do this kind of thing on a typical tour."

Cody shook his head slowly, eyes narrowed. "You can be damn sure of that."

Carol looked at him. His rough voice had an edge

to it, sensual yet forbidding. It made her want to run back, throw her arms around him, and try that again. She wanted to see if it really had been as good as it seemed, as exciting, as breathtaking! But common sense won out. The Jeep was the safest place to be.

By the time he climbed in next to her, she was ready for him. She turned to face him, eyes cool as ice. "That's forgotten, right?"

When he didn't answer, she pushed him. "I mean it, Cody. I don't want any trouble. All I want is a tour."

He nodded, making a sound deep in his throat that was too harsh for laughter. "Forgotten it is," he drawled. "The last thing I want is more trouble." He jerked the Jeep into gear and took off, raising a plume of dust behind them.

Driving seemingly by remote control, he showed her Lost Gulch and Horseshoe Canyon. He drove down an old dry wash, the Jeep rattling so hard, Carol was sure the wheels would fall off, and into a valley where the tall cliff walls threw dark shadows on the valley floor. Stopping in front of a curved section of buff-colored sandstone, he pointed out the petroglyphs carved there: Deer and hunters frozen in timeless pursuit. Further up the valley he stopped again to show her the small stone rooms carved into the cliff-side, granaries and storehouses built by the long-vanished Anasazi. He pointed to the purple shadow of a far-off mountain. "The Apache fled there when the whites tried to force them off their land."

"Were they able to stay?"

"No," Cody said softly. "But they fought hard for it. They loved this land, they and the Navajo, the Pueblo, the Southern Utes . . . all the tribes. They believe the land is sacred, that it's a part of who we are and that a person's relationship to the land defines them and makes them whole."

"And you? What do you believe?"

"Me?" He looked at her as if weighing what to say, how to say it, then suddenly a shadow fell behind his eyes. He shrugged, the corner of his mouth turning down in a cold smile. "Wrong tour. This three-hour version offers only the scenery."

He jammed the Jeep into gear again and drove on, seemingly impervious to the jolts and bounces that made Carol's teeth rattle in her head.

"Okay," she said, grabbing his upper arm, her fingers digging into his flesh through the material of his T-shirt. "I give. Enough names and places. I'm ready to go back. You've proven your point."

Then why did he feel like hell? As quickly as it had seized him, his anger faded. He wanted her to see the beauty of this place he loved, to sense its magic. Instead he was behaving like some spurned teenager. Damn, she had him turned inside out. But it wasn't too late.

"One more stop. It will be worth it, I promise."

He drove the steep road up to Overlook Point and parked. Not satisfied with the flat, railed overhang where the tourists usually stood, Cody scrambled up some boulders with the surefooted ease of a wild creature, his dark hair flying. Smiling down at her, he offered a hand. "Come on. This is a highlight of the tour, a Briggs's special. Can't have you missing it, can we?"

He pulled her up next to him, dropping an arm across her shoulders in a seemingly casual gesture as if his only motive were to steady her on the boulder's rough surface. With his free hand he pointed toward the hazy distance. "See that dark shape out there? That's Mingus Mountain. Beyond that lies the Verde Valley. And if you went straight north, you'd be crossing the Mogollon Rim to the San Francisco Peaks, and beyond that waits the Grand Canyon." He spoke softly, his arm laying lightly on her shoulder, the whole side of her body pressed against his, making it almost impossible for Carol to follow his travelogue, but his next words rang clear. "If you could fly like an eagle, you'd see the history of the earth spread out below you."

Carol had been hypnotized by his nearness, his heat. Now she suddenly pulled away. *Fly like an eagle . . . ?* She felt dizzy, the world spinning. The words, the image evoked her mystical dream. Putting a hand out for balance, she sank down onto the warm rock, brushed the hair back from her face, and narrowed her eyes. "I think I'll stay right here on earth, thank you."

He frowned down at her. "Are you okay?"

"Fine." She pointed her stare off toward the horizon.

Cody hunkered down next to her. "You're really an expert at that, aren't you? You can pull that wall up between you and the world whenever you want. I should take lessons."

"You?" Carol gave a soft snort of derision.

"I can be hurt too," he said softly. He looked away, but not before she caught the flicker of pain in his eyes.

It surprised her, disarmed her. But years of repression kept her mute. She shrugged and slid off the rock, sneakers hitting the sand with a soft thump. "I'm going to take a picture from the overlook," she announced. "Back in a minute."

Cody watched her walk away toward the overlook. She was a slim, golden figure etched against the blue haze of the distance. She didn't look real. Standing there, sun-drenched and shining, she seemed to be made of pure light, ethereal, otherworldly. If he reached for her, she'd disappear . . . or change into something that could tear his heart out. Again the power of his vision swept through him. His heart was pounding in his chest like a drum.

When she started back, he leapt down from the rocks with the sure animal grace of a mountain lion and strode off toward the Jeep. "We'd better get back. It's getting late."

"All right." She sighed, turning to face the blue mountains on the horizon again. "Though I hate to go. I love it up here. I have to admit I've loved the whole trip. It's not at all what I expected. It's . . . it's beautiful, and amazing. I thought the desert was the desert, and that was all. You've shown me a whole world."

Cody flinched as if a hand had closed around his heart. The muscles jumped along his jaw. He stopped and stared at her.

Carol shook her head, a rueful smile tipping her lips. "It doesn't matter what I say, does it? It's always the wrong thing. But for what you've shown me, I forgive even your bad temper and your moods. I'm willing to chalk that all up to some . . . I don't know, some bad chemistry between just the two of us. Other people do say nice things about you."

"Good. As long as you're satisfied. I need this work."

"Yes, you said that before. Well, then you can work." She shrugged. "The Ocotillo can certainly use a good tour guide."

"Thank you."

Carol sank down against a rock and lifted the damp hair off the back of her neck. "You can thank me by letting the tour run a few minutes late. I want to sit here in the shade and look around for a few minutes more, okay? I think the sun's finally got to me. I'm exhausted."

"Whatever you say, boss."

She laughed. "Glad we finally got *that* settled! You were tough to tame."

Something flickered like a flame behind his dark eyes, but he only grinned back at her. "I can be that way. It's a real problem."

Carol let her head fall back and closed her eyes. She heard his footsteps disappear into the distance. A moment later she heard the soft, sweet sound of a flute. It sounded like the voice of the wind, like voices calling across the vast distance of time. It stopped, and there was the low, husky sound of a song, a man's deep, melodious voice rising and falling.

She opened her eyes a fraction, just enough to let a little light in, and then her heart skipped a beat. Cody was standing at the very edge of the cliff, a dark shape against the bright whiteness of the noon light filling the canyon, and then that dark shape moved, shifted, changed! Was there a wolf there, a mountain lion, *an eagle*?

Carol's mouth went dry, and then there was the bitter, coppery taste of fear. She said softly, "Cody?"

In the shimmer of the light the shape turned toward her.

She called again, louder. "Cody?"

And then the shape took form, became Cody Briggs, walking slowly toward her from the edge of the cliff, his dark hair lifting in the wind, his body moving with a wild, fierce grace. "What is it? Something wrong?"

"Nothing. Nothing's wrong. What were you doing?"

He shrugged, a lift of broad-muscled shoulders. "I was retelling one of the old legends . . . an old Navajo story. They're meant to be chanted, and I like the sound of them out in all this emptiness. Why?"

"I don't know. I thought . . ." She laughed, brushing away the memory with a wave of her hand. "For a second you looked strange over there."

"And now?" He grinned down at her.

"Still strange, but definitely you." She gave another little laugh, weak with relief. "I just don't understand how you can be bothered with all of that nonsense, chanting and stuff—"

"It's not nonsense, Lonesome. It's beautiful. Powerful. These songs and legends have served a culture well for thousands of years. The Navajo believe they keep the world in balance, in harmony, and allow you to walk in the path of beauty. Looking at the rest of the world today, I'd say they've got a pretty good idea going. A lot more valuable than filling up hotel rooms at three hundred and fifty dollars a night."

That stung. "I notice you're awfully anxious to get your piece of the pie, aren't you, Briggs? You just spent the whole day begging for a job."

"Is that what I did?" he asked, his voice low and dangerous. For just a second she actually expected him to shift shape, to become whatever she'd imagined and gobble her up, but all he did was brush past her and stalk down the path to the Jeep.

What an ending for this crazy morning. Carol couldn't figure out what emotion she was feeling most . . . anger or lust. Worse, she couldn't figure out why she even cared.

FIVE

The afternoon stretched on endlessly. Sitting alone with old memories tearing at her heart from one side while the raw memory of Cody Briggs and their strange morning tore at her from the other was like being caught between a rock and a hard place. Carol wearily gave up on her feeble attempt to relax. Work was easier.

Slipping into a pale cream linen dress, she walked over to the hotel. She could see her stand-in's head bent over her ledger, the concierge desk sitting like a calm oasis in the middle of the lobby. Avoiding the display cases and their shadowed corner, Carol stepped briskly over to the desk.

"Hi, Edna, I'm back. There are a few things I'd like to work on and the front desk is fully staffed, so why don't you take the afternoon off."

"Really?" the Navajo woman said cheerfully. "That would be wonderful, Ms. Lawson. My uncle,

Charlie Yazzie, is making a sing for his new baby, and I would like to help with the cooking."

"A 'sing'?" Carol repeated, interested.

"It's a Navajo religious ceremony," Edna explained. "We believe that all the universe, good and bad, exists in harmony. All things are connected. When a baby is born the family makes a sing, a 'Blessingway,' to help that child be part of the harmony. We say, the child will 'walk in beauty.'"

"You should go, by all means," Carol said quickly, struggling to keep her face smooth. Inside she felt a sharp stab of pain. But she held a smile as Edna got up from behind the desk. "I'll see you in the morning. Have a lovely sing."

"Yes. Thank you."

It was as if the weight of her sorrow dragged Carol down into her chair. For just a second the world swam. That's how it always happened: Suddenly, without warning, with unbearable pain. It could be a story on TV, a picture in the newspaper, a single word: *Baby*. Grief shook her by the hair. Now she had to blink hard to fight back the tears. What in the world had happened to her calm, perfect oasis?

Shrugging hard, as if she could physically throw off the weight suffocating her, Carol opened the ledger and began to check off guest names against charge slips. Later she'd do some work on the operations manual she was developing for the Ocotillo based on the same format she'd used in Atlanta. That's what had gotten her this promotion, good ideas and good hard work, and the combination would carry her to success here too. And if the sadness got too bad, she'd just work harder, and *harder*. There was a point where if she got tired enough, even the past faded. Then she could sleep. If she had to, she knew how to get there.

Head bent, Carol checked every tour scheduled for the rest of the week, read through two brochures that had come in from new hot-air balloon companies, called and spoke to their owners, selecting one, rejecting the other, and then began work on section two of her manual: Improving guest relations through personnel training.

A shadow fell across her desk. Her heart stopped. *Cody?* She had to close her eyes for a moment before she could dare to look up. But when she did, it was a middle-aged man in golf clothes, leaning his golf bag against the front edge of her desk.

"Hi there. Didn't mean to startle you."

"You didn't, of course not. May I help you?"

"I'm Russ Howard. But you're not the same person I spoke to earlier," he stated, frowning.

"That must have been Ms. Yazzie. I'm Carol Lawson, the assistant manager," she said, standing and shaking hands. "Please sit down. Is there something I can do for you?"

"You betcha. I've got to have a tour with Doctor Briggs. Now I know—" he rushed on, talking right over Carol's sound of dismay. "I know that Ms. Yazzie said that Doctor Briggs is unavailable. But this is important. I was here in the spring and I'm back again, and Cody Briggs is the reason why."

Well, Carol thought in confusion, at least they were talking about the same man. But *Doctor Briggs?*

"Of course," she repeated, stalling for time. "Let me just make sure I understand. You went on a tour with him last spring—"

"Yes. April. Just after all the controversy. Heck, their loss was certainly my gain. I have never spent a day like that, not in my entire life. It reminded me of some of those lectures on metaphysics I sat through my freshman year at Yale, feeling like someone was finally giving me the key to understanding the universe. And there we were, just him and me, right out in the middle of the desert. Incredible. You know that feeling, don't you?"

"Oh yes," she whispered, her heart tightening as she saw that beautiful body magically shift and change shape, feeling again the power of his touch, his kiss . . . "Yes, I know that feeling."

"Good. Then you understand why I must have a tour. I won't take no for an answer."

"But Mr. Howard—"

"Congressman Howard. If that'll help get me a tour with Doctor Briggs, I'm willing to discard modesty."

"Congressman. I'm sorry, I didn't recognize your name."

"No harm done . . . unless you don't book that tour. Then I'm liable to raise your taxes—personally!"

Carol gave him an appreciative smile, though her head was spinning. "I will certainly do my best."

"As Captain Picard says, 'Make it so!'" With a smile he hefted his golf bag and was gone.

Carol got up stiffly from behind the desk. Pressing one hand to her throat, she stared out into the pale golden sunlight of late afternoon, then back into the shadowed corner of the lobby.

What was going on here?

She edged over, not knowing exactly what was causing the tremor of fear in her stomach. Did she expect Cody to leap out at her from the dimness? Did she think an eagle would stir to life from a display shelf, swoop down, and steal her away?

Stopping at the first case, she looked at a row of wooden statues, vividly painted, decorated with feathers and beads, posed midstep in some mystical dance. The card read: *Hopi Kachina dolls used during the Powamu, or Bean Dance ceremony. Private collection: C. Briggs.* Below those was a grouping of rawhide drums, beautifully painted. *Private Collection: C. Briggs.* There were tall, curved bows and stone-tipped arrows in beaded quivers, their threads unraveled by years and use, and old Navajo saddle trimmings worked in silver and inlaid with turquoise. The middle case held a row of seventeenth century woven baskets, pottery shards, and a dozen ancient grinding stones worn to dark smoothness by the hands of the long-vanished cliff-dwelling Anasazi. *Private collection: C. Briggs.* Carol touched one fingertip to the glass. Her hand was shaking. The last case held magnificent feathered replicas of the Zuni war gods, then three shelves of Zuni fetishes and their accompanying fetish jars and bowls. This card read: *"The Zuni have a complex religion that permeates every aspect of their lives. Ceremonials assure that the rains will fall, harvests will be bountiful, and the life of the people will be long and happy."* *Artifacts on loan from a private collection.*

Cody Briggs. Chills rippled over Carol's skin. She'd never even stopped to look at these ancient beautiful things; she'd let herself be driven away by her fear of shadows and mystery. Now she felt their power. They stirred unexpected emotions to life deep within her soul.

Again a shiver rippled through her, but this time it was accompanied by a strange heat coiled at the base of her belly. That's what Cody did to her. His dark beauty and mystery lured her with the same unfathomable power. And he had secrets too. The thought was a powerful intoxicant, and it evoked the image of him there at the edge of her vision, just beyond her reach, a shadow within the shadows. From the moment he had stepped from that darkness he had held her, fascinated her, drawn her to him. Now she was going to know why.

She called the tour office, but Cody was gone. She left a message and sat waiting, trying to work, feeling her heart flutter.

And then, as if she'd conjured him up out of the shadows and the bright desert light, there was Cody Briggs, striding toward her.

Hat pulled low so that only the chiseled line of his jaw was clearly visible, duster swinging from his broad shoulders, holster clinched around lean hips, boots already dusty with desert sand . . . He ate up the distance between them. Tossing his hat on her desk, he swept a hand through his hair. "So . . . you want me?"

And how! Carol thought before she could stop herself.

She had to catch her breath before she could formulate an answer. It had to be the effect of the old artifacts with their strange magic, the heat, her confusion and tiredness. What else could it be that kept her from breathing?

When there wasn't a drop of air left in her lungs, she parted her lips and drew in a deep breath. That burst of oxygen was fuel for all sorts of flames.

"Who are you, Cody? What the heck is going on? You come on like some down-and-out cowboy who needs a job, some desert renegade with the soul of a poet. You drive me crazy, take up my day off . . . and then I find out you're a doctor? A doctor, for Pete's sake! I want to know what's going on."

Pushing aside her paperwork, he settled one hip on her desk. The muscles in his flank and thigh strained against the worn denim of his jeans. "What are you doing here, Carol? Couldn't find anything more interesting to do with the rest of your day off?"

"That's none of your business," she snapped, trying to keep her eyes off his muscle-stretched jeans. "And don't change the subject. Tell me who you are."

"I'm Cody Briggs," he answered with maddening nonchalance.

"*Doctor* Cody Briggs?"

He shrugged, the corner of his mouth tugging down in a flicker of a grin. "That too."

"Great. What kind of doctor? Medical, professional, *theological*—" she drawled, leaning toward him across the desk, her blue eyes flashing with irritation.

He gave a low, husky laugh and pushed the hair back from her cheek. "Your eyes turn almost violet when you're angry, Lonesome. You're very beautiful."

Carol drew back, her cheek aflame where he had touched her. "You're impossible."

Cody shrugged. "It all depends on how one defines the possible."

Carol shut her eyes. She had to close out the sight of him for one moment and clear her thoughts.

Cody felt a sudden jolt of longing rocket to his groin. It was the way her lashes lay against her cheek, a soft curve of harmony between feathery lash and silken skin. It was the vulnerable loveliness of her, the beauty of which she seemed so unaware shadowed by the sadness in her soul. He groaned silently, fighting the hot ache in his loins. At least he understood *that* pain. What he didn't understand was why his heart was aching so. Trouble was, if he didn't want her so desperately, he wouldn't have to torment her so brutally.

Uncoiling from her desk, he spoke in a voice made rough by impatience. "I've got to get going. If you want any more answers, we'll have to talk another time."

Carol blinked, startled by the sudden rush of cold air against her chest where his body heat had been. At least she was safe with him standing dark and remote at the far side of the desk. But if she let him set the rules now, she'd never get the upper hand again.

"You are darn right I want answers. And I'll get them before I let you work here, *Doctor* Briggs. Even if congressmen do come in and ask for you by name."

Cody relaxed, smiling now. "Who was it? Russ Howard? Is that what got you all steamed up?"

Carol gave a soft little laugh of disbelief and leaned back, lips parted in a smile. "'Steamed up?'" she drawled, dismissing the idea as utterly ridiculous. "I simply think people should be honest with each other . . . in a business relationship *especially*," she added quickly, seeing his dark eyes narrow challengingly. She slid a hand under the hair at the back of her neck, lifted it, then let it fall slowly, wishing she was somewhere else . . . anywhere else. "Anyway, what shall I tell Congressman Howard?"

"Sign him up," Cody answered with a shrug. "If I'm working for you, then put me to work."

"Okay. Fine. I will."

"Great. Now, if that takes care of all your problems—" Before she knew it he was striding away, about to vanish again into that bright desert light.

"Wait. I never did get the answers I want." She was leaning forward, shoulders set, frowning, needing to have the last word.

"You want more answers, come out to my camp tonight—"

"Your camp?" Carol interrupted with a laugh. "Oh, no thank you. I am not wandering out to some 'camp,' whatever that means. I can *only* guess. Besides, what's a doctor doing hanging out in some camp?"

"You'd prefer a condo in Scottsdale? A penthouse in Phoenix?"

"I'd prefer something normal. Something sensible."

"Then you've got the wrong guy."

"I don't 'have' *any* guy," Carol snapped, the words coming out before she could stop them.

"Want one?" Cody was back, leaning over her desk with a wild, daring grin.

Carol tipped up her chin. "If I did, it would be a sweet Southern gentleman with good manners."

Cody gave an appreciative, husky laugh. "That was a gotcha, huh? Well," He leaned forward, resting both hands flat on her desk. "All I can say is that it strikes me mighty funny you moved from Georgia to Arizona, if that's what you're looking for. Me . . . I think you don't know yet what you want. Or are afraid to admit it." With a wink he slapped his hat against his thigh and turned to leave.

"Cody?" Carol said softly before she even knew she would. That's what he did to her: Either caught the words in her throat or had them popping out before she could stop them. "I . . . I just wanted you to know I looked at the things in the display cases."

He stopped and turned, his dark eyes softened now with a strange and unexpected tenderness. "I was wondering how long it was going to take for them to reach you. They're beautiful, aren't they?"

"Yes." She nodded, sensing the incredible passion

his words masked, just as she had felt the passion he had tried to hide from her moments before. *Secrets . . .* she thought ruefully. *I'm far too familiar with secrets, and you're not nearly as good at hiding them as I am.* She dropped her gaze, swiveling her chair to face the display cases. "They are very beautiful. Mystical almost."

"In a way, yes," he replied, standing close now. "What I feel is a great awe. A reverence. I think of the hands that carved them, painted them, wove them. I think of the beliefs that were sustained and celebrated, the diverse but beautiful cultures they represent, cultures vanished or changed by time and history. I think of the men, women, or children who held each one in their hands and tried to live in harmony and balance with a world that would change so drastically around them." He paused and looked down at her, and a self-effacing grin lit his handsome face. "I do go on, don't I?"

"You're a teacher, aren't you? A professor?" Carol said softly. "It's a Ph.D. that makes you 'Doctor' Briggs, right?"

"Right," he said, a sudden sharpness edging his voice. With a frown he turned his head so that all she saw was his profile, sharp and eagle-fierce. "At least the Ph.D. is right. The teaching part has . . . changed."

"Why?"

It was as if she touched an exposed nerve. His head jerked up; a muscle jumped at the clenched angle of his jaw. Eyes narrowed, he turned back to glare at her as if somehow she was responsible for the pain that cut through him. Then he got control of himself and shook his head. "I told you. For any more answers you'll have to come to my camp tonight."

"And I told you I wouldn't."

"Fine." He shrugged, grinning as though her stubbornness excited him somehow. He looked at her for a second, a gaze as intent as the one he had lavished on the artifacts, but tinged with more lust than reverence. "Come late. After dark. I run first, on the mesa top at sunset. Habit. But later . . . I'll wait for you."

"Don't!" she replied automatically, stunned by the realization that *he* was the man she'd seen running bare-chested across the mesa that first evening . . . or was it before that? Had he been in her dream . . . ? But how? Why?

With a shiver Carol pulled herself back to the present. This was crazy. She wouldn't even let him *think* she was the kind of woman to go wandering around the desert in the dark in search of some sexy, unpredictable hunk of a man. Ha! "Besides . . ." she snapped, "how would I get there?"

"Straight as an arrow out toward the mesa, in an arroyo with a clump of cottonwood. I'll have a fire burning."

I'll have a fire burning . . . The words were laced with innuendo, recognition of which blazed in his ebony eyes. Trouble was, a fire was already burning deep at the core of her body, flamed by his teasing grin.

She pressed her lips together. "I meant *how* would I get there? How far is it?"

"Here," he said, sliding his fingers into the front pocket of his jeans. "Here are the keys to the Jeep. I'll walk back."

"No, don't be silly. Take them. I'm not going to use them."

He dropped them into her lap. "See ya later, Lonesome. I'll be there if you want me."

SIX

The flames danced in the darkness. Red and gold, leaping and writhing, they could have been the souls of ancient warriors painted for battle, burning fierce and pure at their hearts. Cody could almost hear the drums.

He had been waiting for hours, and he was explosive with anger . . . at himself for wanting her to come and at Carol for not appearing when he desired it so much. He was cruelly aware of the hunger building inside him, the fierce raging of his pulse. Why had he let this happen? Why had he invited her to this private place? Why did he even consider letting her close to his soul? A year before he had closed the door on trust and candor, those foolish virtues. He knew better now. He'd found a new way to live in this world, and it included not trusting anyone.

With a growl he snapped another branch in two and fed it to the flames. Damn! Hadn't he learned a

damn thing this last year? Hadn't he already lost everything a man could lose: His job? his friends? the
world's respect? his future? *What was left?*

With a laugh rough with bitterness, he felt the
answer crumble to ashes in his chest. *His heart.* Oh
God, it hurt. He thought he'd gone beyond pain to
the dry desert of isolation. Alone, just doing a simple
job, he thought he was safe. And then she'd come,
Carol Lawson, carrying some secret pain that somehow reached into his own soul. Lonesome. Lovely
and brave and silent. Why did he want so desperately
to break through the wall she'd built? Why did he
ache for her to appear in the darkness?

Groaning, he ran his fingers through his hair and
stared into the fire, seeking peace, seeking oblivion.
Moving closer, Cody hunkered down and wrapped his
arms around his knees. The muscles of his buttocks,
thighs, and calves tightened, straining against the
denim of his jeans. He was bare-chested. The desert
air was still warm on his broad back and shoulders;
the fire shadows played across the hard, smooth muscles of his chest and belly. Long black hair fell over
his face, accenting the hard line of cheek and jaw.

He closed his eyes and used his power to clear his
mind. As the heat played across his skin, Cody lost
himself in the hiss and snap of the fire. When he
opened his eyes, it was to see only the flames, blue
and burning at their heart.

And then he saw *her*. Or he seemed to see her,
though no one had stepped near to break the trance.
He saw Carol standing on the far side of the fire, the

flames lifting her from shadow to light then hiding her again. She was beautiful . . . more than beautiful. She was ethereal, dreamlike, yet more real to him at the moment than his own flesh and muscle. Her eyes were shining in the firelight: Round and thick-lashed, they pierced him with a pure blue flame of longing. Her body seemed to tremble, and the thin, almost transparent dress she wore stirred, clinging to her at breast, belly, and hip.

In that gesture that was so her own, as if she had to hold herself together, she touched her fingers to her breast. He could hear her heart beat like a drum. He felt it beating beneath her fingertips. As if their bodies became one, he felt the warmth of her skin, its silken texture; he felt her nipples peak and tighten against the feathery gauze, aching with the heat of desire; he felt the heat gather between her breasts, climb the fragile column of her throat, and flush her cheeks; he felt a different heat, wild and burning, deep within her body.

An answering desire stirred his loins. He grew hard and eager, aching to touch her, hold her, fill her. He longed to gentle the fear right out of her, to banish whatever hurt held her captive, to free her, and then claim her for his own. Suddenly it was as if some wild creature had entered his skin, and it was that wild, primitive, untamed passion that shifted into his shape and possessed him. He was a creature of earth and sky, moon and wind, as elemental as the fire itself.

Carol? he breathed through dry lips.

Cody? Her answer was a whisper carried by the wind. *Cody, is that you?*

In surreal slow motion, her fingers drifted down her body, stirring the thin pale fabric of her dress. Beneath it her body was taut with tension, thrumming with desire. She touched herself lightly, as if surprised by her own passion, and a fierce surge of desire shot through Cody, squeezing the air out of his lungs. He stared at her hungrily through the flames, and then he saw her emotions change: Her eyes flew wide, her lips rounded in an *O* of pain and surprise; tears clung to her lashes. *Cody?* she whispered, her voice reed thin and almost lost among the snap and pop of sparks. Her hands were opened up in front of her, her palms empty, holding nothing but air. *Cody? I'm frightened. I'm lost and frightened. Empty. I've lost it. Everything . . . everything. Oh Cody, help me. Save me.* And she slowly stepped into the flames.

Cody leapt to his feet, his hands outstretched to stop her, and only the sound of her voice kept him from being burned.

"Cody?" Carol called again, louder this time. His sudden leap toward the fire had scared the hell out of her.

She had been watching him for a full five minutes, mesmerized by the sight of him just as he seemed to be mesmerized by whatever he saw in the flames. He was beautiful, bronze-skinned and dark-eyed. His body seemed to shift back and forth between wild creature and perfectly sculpted man. Carol's hands tingled with the desire to touch him. Every nerve in her body burned with the fever of that desire: To run her hands over his skin, to feel the shape and heat and hardness of every muscle . . . *every* muscle, especially the hot power of his sex thrusting against her, filling her.

Oh Lord, she hadn't allowed herself thoughts like that for nine years. Why now?

But the answer seemed to be there at the back of her mind, and in her chest where her heart beat so wildly against her ribs. Something she didn't understand drew her, consumed her, just as the fire seemed to consume the very air between them. She could leap right through the flames and touch him and he'd be real, *more* than real: Solid and strong and beautiful, not at all like the ghosts and demons that haunted her. He'd be strong enough to protect her, to save her, to banish the terrible dreams, to chase away the grief. In his arms perhaps she could live again, love again, laugh again. *Oh, Cody! Cody . . . !* Tears stung her eyes and clung unshed to her lashes. She trembled with fear and longing. *Cody . . . help me. Save me.*

At the instant she had that thought, Cody had uncoiled and seemed to leap at the flames, stopped midair by Carol's startled cry.

"Cody? Are you all right?"

He shook his head, trying to clear the vision from his foggy brain.

Reality and illusion were blurred together, shifting back and forth in the dance of the flames. Then the world took shape around him, solidified, and the night was filled with silence, the air was growing cool on his shoulders, and Carol was glaring at him, dressed not in gauze and dream, but in stone-washed denim jeans and a pale blue button-down cotton shirt. No nonsense. A lovely vision still, but the magic was gone.

"You're later than I expected," he said. His cool smile was all the welcome she got.

Carol dug his car keys out of her hip pocket. She threw them at him, aiming for his chest. "That's because your lousy Jeep broke down. Back there," she added, tossing her head in the direction from which she'd come. "I had to walk the rest of the damn way—"

"But you found me."

"I figured you were closer than the hotel. Besides, the fire was easy to see." She shrugged, then caught her elbows in her hands. "It's cooler than I expected out here."

"That's the desert. It holds the sun's heat during the day, but at night, between elevation and lack of cloud cover, the temperature drops and—"

"Thank you, Doctor Briggs," Carol said sarcastically, but the edge was gone from her voice, the anger subsided. She stuffed her hands into her pockets and smiled at him.

Cody felt his heart tighten. "Sorry. I tend to do that."

"That's okay. Actually, for some strange reason, I like it." She hesitated a second. "Why did you give up teaching?"

He met her eyes, his own dark glance revealing a

flash of both stubbornness and pain. "I haven't. Obviously." He gave a short, harsh laugh. "Just lost my classroom."

"How?"

"It's a long story. And not very interesting."

"I'm interested," she persisted, stepping around the circumference of the fire's heat until she stood just a few feet from him. The urge to touch him returned with shocking force, catching her breath in her throat. She could reach out her hand and stroke his bare forearm with its long carved muscles and smooth dusky skin, feel the soft dusting of black hair brush against her fingertips. . . .

Dropping her gaze, she saw scattered on the ground a number of small stone triangles. "What are these?" she asked, crouching down quickly to pick one up. It was wafer thin and weightless in her palm, but sharp enough to hurt.

"Arrowheads," Cody muttered, couching beside her, his thigh just inches from the tempting blue line of hers. His fingers grazed her palm as he turned the thin stone triangle over in her hand. "I was practicing while I waited for you. It's easier than it looks, once you master the technique, and there's something calming about the simplicity of the task."

"And you needed calming?" she asked, glancing sideways at him. Her eyes were blue sparks in the darkness, mysterious, thrilling.

Cody drew his tongue over dry lips. "I don't understand it myself." His voice was low and husky; his breath stirred her hair.

Carol felt her skin go cold, then hot. Nothing made sense. Only the tiny stone in her hand was understandable. "Did the Indians around here make arrowheads like these?"

Cody nodded. He stood for just a moment, drawing something from the front pocket of his jeans. "Here. This one I've been carrying around for years. It's an old arrowhead, probably Sioux."

The feel of it in her palm was surprising. It seemed to settle there, warm and alive against her skin. And for an instant, or less, she *saw* an old Indian warrior, white-haired, in a fancy buckskin shirt . . .

She blinked and the image was gone.

"What is it?" Cody asked, watching her face.

"Nothing." She laughed quickly. "Although the feel of it is somehow . . . I don't know, *familiar*."

"Maybe you were a warrior in another life," Cody said with a grin. His fingers played against her open palm. "Maybe you were—"

Carol lost track of his words, aware only of the heat of his touch. She dropped the stone chip back into his palm. "Enough about arrowheads. Tell me why you're not teaching, Cody."

He looked at her a moment, his dark eyes hooded and remote, then straightened and offered her a hand up. She rose, dusting off the back of her jeans with her free hand. The other was tucked into his. As he began to speak, she could feel the tension in his fingers; his grip was not tight enough to hurt her, but almost.

"I got fired. Dismissed. Thrown out on my ass.

Everyone I knew, everyone I trusted at the university, people I'd worked with for years . . . every one of them turned their backs on me and buried their heads in the sand. Some of them—" he snorted in derision —"may even have secretly applauded, though they were careful enough not to do it to my face."

"What happened?" Carol asked softly.

His hand tightened convulsively, but his face remained unreadable, carved in stone like the arrowheads. "I did what I had to do. What nobody else would do."

"Sounds like you, Briggs."

He shrugged, the corner of his mouth tugged upward in a grimace that bore only faint resemblance to a smile. "Never was too big on college politics."

"What are you big on?"

"Doing what's right." He dropped her hand and dug his own through his hair in a weary, bitter gesture. "Listen, Carol, I don't feel like—"

"Don't even say it, Briggs. I drove out here . . . I *walked* out here, because . . . because," she repeated softly, "you promised to tell me. You can't welsh on the deal now. Your integrity rating would be zero."

He studied her from behind his lashes. She could see the pain in his face, lines of hurt and betrayal illuminated by the fire's glow. His broad chest was rising and falling, and she could almost see the pounding of that fierce, angry heart.

Feeling her gaze on him, Cody took a step back into darkness. But still he couldn't escape her. With a shrug of capitulation, he dug the old arrowhead out of his pocket again. He looked at it as if he, too, were receiving some kind of vision, a vision that tormented him. Yet his voice was steady and low. "I'm an archeologist and a cultural anthropologist. That's who I am. I started when I was a kid, poking around in the dirt in Minnesota, hunting for arrowheads, pottery shards, burial mounds. I had a Sioux great-grandfather; the rest of the family was Norwegian and Celt, a little Italian thrown in for spice. But that great-grandfather . . . he was the one who fascinated me. Maybe because he was lost in the mists of history. For everyone else there was a Bible, a birth certificate, but him . . . there was only his spirit reaching across all that time and distance. And even then I knew that was what was important. *To not lose that spirit, that trust.* That's what I've worked for my whole life.

"I got my doctorate, taught at the university, wrote books . . . and I loved it. I loved what I did, what I learned, what I taught. And I loved unearthing the old things: An arrowhead, a piece of pottery, a mask or a bowl or a knife. Each one was attached to a way of life that has either vanished or is in danger of extinction. Each one was sacred." He paused, swallowing around a dry throat, then struggled on.

"I was head of the cultural-anthro department at the university. Responsible for the artifacts unearthed by university-sponsored digs as well as my class load. We . . . three *colleagues* and I . . ." He spit out the word colleagues as if it were poison on his tongue. ". . . we had assembled a show that was bound for the Denver Museum of Natural History, then on to the Smithsonian. Just before it was to be shipped out I discovered that some of the things were missing. *Sacred* things. Things that deserved respect if not reverence, things beyond value." The muscles jumped along the knife-sharp line of his jaw. His voice dropped to a growl. "I couldn't believe it. They'd been sold. For cash. A lot of cash. I never could locate them. Some private collector is sitting with a Yei mask on his living room wall because another teacher—a friend, someone I trusted—wanted a few more bucks in his bank account, or a BMW in his garage." In the firelight, Cody's face looked dark and dangerous. Sweat beaded his forehead.

"What happened?"

Cody gave a grunt of derision. His lip curled in a sardonic smile. "Not much. A little tidying up and it was all over, just needed to let the dust settle."

"But you lost your job—"

"You 'lose' a watch, a wallet. They took my job away."

"But why? *You* hadn't done anything wrong."

Cody tossed a handful of twigs into the fire, making the sparks fly. He slid her a dark, hooded glance. "Let's say I didn't turn out to be the right kind of 'team player.'"

If she was hoping for a better explanation than that, she was sorely disappointed. Without another word Cody uncoiled and stood, feet apart, hands planted on his lean hips. "I'll make us a cup of coffee."

Carol hurried to her feet, following him out of the

circle of light. "Thanks anyway, but I don't want a cup of coffee. You can't end the story there, Briggs."

He turned on her, eyes blazing. "Like hell. I can do whatever I damn please now. And who are you—" He backed her toward the fire one step at a time, his eyes burning into hers. ". . . who are *you* to dig into my soul? What about you, Lonesome? What secrets are *you* hiding?"

Carol tripped on a branch and sat down hard, the air escaping her lungs in a soft little "oof" of panic. "We're not talking about me, Cody."

"Why not? Why don't we ever talk about you, Carol? What do I even know about you? That I'm drawn to you for some reason that I can't even begin to explain, but can't seem to resist? That you come from Atlanta and like to bury yourself in work. That you're sad in the way I'm sad, but worse . . . and that scares the hell out of me. When I look in your beautiful eyes and see that sorrow, that fear, it tears my guts out—"

"Then don't look." Carol pivoted on her bottom and faced the fire, arms crossed over her breasts. When she heard him move closer, she scrambled to her feet. "Cody, I came out here tonight because I was curious. I told you that. I didn't mean to pry, not really. I don't believe in that. I can't."

"Why not?"

"Because . . . because I'm a very private person. Cautious. Wary . . ." She ran out of breath and shook her head, eyes lowered. "I shouldn't have come."

"Maybe not."

"Fine. Then I'll go now."

"Good idea." He kicked sand at the fire, and sparks leapt into the darkness.

Carol stared at him, pale brows drawn down in confusion and frustration. "I can't believe this. Are you really not going to tell me the rest of your story, Briggs?"

Muttering something Carol considered in extremely bad taste, Cody strode off. She heard the clatter of tin pans. "What are you doing?"

"Making that cup of coffee."

"Don't make any for me. I told you I don't want—"

"Then you can take it and—"

There was the loud, unmistakable sound of a throat being cleared in the darkness, and then a man stepped out from behind a saguaro. "*Ahalani.* Greetings, Cody. Nice night."

Carol jumped.

Cody slid his hand down from the knife belted at his hip. "Greetings yourself. Another move like that, and I'll be at your mother's hogan, singing your soul back to the Creator. What are you doing out here?"

The stranger hesitated, glancing at Carol. "I thought I'd just stop out and talk awhile. But—" His tone lightened. "Catching the tail end of your conversation when I rode up reminded me how much I've missed your charming company *and* your easygoing ways." More relaxed now, he winked at Carol, who couldn't help but smile back.

Cody scowled at her. "Don't encourage him. Carol Lawson, this is Leonard John. Leonard, Carol."

"Well, it's about time." Leonard held out a hand as he gave Carol a friendly, but openly appraising stare. "So *you're* her. I wondered what you'd be like." Then he tipped his chin toward the tense, silent figure looming in the darkness. "I'm Cody's brother in the Navajo Nation. His friend, his student . . . and sometimes his teacher. He hasn't mentioned me?"

"I'm afraid not," Carol answered, knowing the man wasn't the least bit surprised. "It must have been a momentary oversight."

"Ah yes. That . . . or the fact that Cody Briggs can sometimes be a man of too few words. Obviously the problem he's having this evening."

"Leonard—" Cody warned.

"Come on, Cody, relax. Brothers can trust each other to do what's right. Come over here by the fire, and we can both explain to Carol—"

"Like hell!" The blood had drained from Cody's face. He turned away. "I've got no explaining to do. If you want to talk, that's your business, but I'm going to scrounge up some old saguaro ribs for the fire." His footsteps crunched angrily off into the desert night.

Carol looked from Cody's forbidding back to the fire to Leonard. "Is it always that difficult to get that man to talk?"

"It depends. Talk about Native American culture and Cody will go on till you want to strangle him. I have spent many a night smoking and yawning and talking until dawn. But if you ask about what happened last year, about how he feels now . . . then there are few words. None for you."

"But why not?" Carol asked softly.

"Because they hurt him. Because to you he wants to be strong and proud, too strong to be hurt. We men have that problem when we wish to win a woman's favor; it doesn't matter if you live in Shiprock or Cincinnati. At least that's what Ray—my wife—says." His voice drifted away.

Pale brows knit in a frown, Carol stared at Leonard. "Will *you* tell me? What did Cody do that got him fired? I can't even imagine. What did he do to jeopardize his job when he obviously loved it so much?"

"He did what was right. I can tell you this only because I have heard the tone of his voice when he speaks of you, and tonight I have seen how he looks at you. For these reasons I can tell you that he put aside what he loved and did what had to be done. He gave the old things back to the tribes."

"He *what?*" Carol gasped, understanding immediately the enormity of that act. "He took some of the artifacts and returned them to the Native Americans?"

"All of them. He said that if the university would not pursue the theft . . . if they would not prosecute and retrieve the stolen pieces because they were afraid of the media coverage . . . if they could allow that sacrilege, then none of the artifacts were safe and they should be returned to the People. It was the right thing to do. At least I believe that."

"But he didn't dare! Not really?"

"Yes."

"So they fired him. Now I understand. But couldn't he get probation, or something—?"

"Nothing unless he agreed to cover it up and beg back the artifacts he'd returned. He said he would go to hell first."

Carol looked around at his campsite: The sleeping bag in the shadows under the lean-to, the camp stove and its two tin cooking pots, the silent desert stretching all around, the stars shining above. "Well, it's not hell, but a far cry from head of a department at a major university."

"It's a nice camp," Leonard said, nodding to himself. "Needs a hogan, a house. And of course a sweat lodge. But otherwise it's not too bad."

"No, I guess not," Carol agreed halfheartedly.

"And of course there's the ranch."

"Ranch?"

"Cody's ranch up near Sedona. It's very beautiful. Set among the red rocks. Good medicine. Very powerful."

Carol drew a deep, steadying breath, then cocked her head to better see Leonard's face. "Could we go over that again. Slowly. If Cody has a ranch, why—?"

"Why is he living here, driving Jeep tours?" Leonard pursed his mouth, wondering how to explain. "I think it is a way to continue to teach about the land and the people he loves. Also, a way to cleanse himself of the guilt he feels for not having better protected the sacred things. I said to him, 'Brother, you were betrayed by people you trusted; it was not your fault.' But it is hard for him to hear me. It may take another voice."

Carol barely heard Leonard's voice. Her senses were being pummeld by the very emotions she had struggled so long to repress: Betrayal, guilt, grief, loss. Oh God, suddenly it was as if her skin were melting in the fire's heat and there was nothing left to hold her together, and her soul were about to float away, a lost, sad little wisp of a thing—*She'd held it in her arms for just a moment, one moment, counting ten little fingers, ten little toes, and then they'd taken it away . . . she'd let it go . . . her arms were empty. And her heart was broken into a thousand pieces and there was nothing but the sound of crying and she didn't know if it was the baby's or her own, but it went on and on. . . .* Carol pressed her hands to her ears.

Out of the desert came the sweet, lilting notes of a flute. The sound had a magic of its own, a bright thread spun from times long past, silver toned and harmonious. She didn't have to ask who made that music.

"Cody," she whispered.

"Yes." Frowning, Leonard stared out into the darkness. "He makes good music. He has the power. That is why I'm here tonight."

Carol heard the strain in his voice. Perhaps she was intruding on something very personal between the two men. Softly she asked, "Is that a Navajo song?"

Leonard looked up this time, into the dark sky. "Our songs and chants are used mostly in our ceremonials. There are curing sings and 'Blessingway' rites, and all are meant to ensure that man can 'walk in beauty.' That is the central concept of the belief of the *Dine´e*, the People: That all parts of the universe are in harmony."

Carol nodded, remembering Edna's words.

"Well, I have taught Cody some of the 'ways' based on our mythology. Partly for his books; partly because I wished to bring harmony back to a friend's life. But what he plays now is a song born within his own heart." Leonard smiled gently. "Do you like it?"

Carol shrugged; habit made her hide her feelings. "I like all music."

Leonard nodded. "Then you might like a story I know. Have you ever heard the story of Hehaka, the Elk? It is a Plains Indian story; Cody told it to my littlest girl one day this summer. Here, sit near the fire and I'll tell you."

As she settled down onto the sand at Leonard's side, the sound of the flute drifted to them again on the cool night breeze. Carol buttoned the top button of her shirt, hugged her elbows with her hands, and listened.

"Well," Leonard began, "Hehaka the elk is very noble, very brave. He puts himself between his herd and the wind, between his herd and the wolves. He has a strong heart, full of courage, worthy of trust.

But, there is something else to know . . . he also has the 'love wink' in his eye.

"Yes," he responded to Carol's startled smile. "Yes. And when he finds the one he wants, the whole forest echoes with his song. His spirit is the flute spirit. *Siyotanka,* the flute. That's for making love."

Carol laughed softly, a shaky little sound high in her throat. She couldn't help herself. It was the night, the darkness, the stars sparkling overhead, the fire snapping. The sound of the flute, mystical and enchanting, was drawing nearer and nearer. When it stopped suddenly, she shivered, and stared into the darkness with wide, unblinking eyes.

SEVEN

The flute fell silent, replaced seconds later by the crunch of boots on sand. Holding a bundle of long, dry saguaro ribs, Cody stepped back into the circle of firelight. With an angry look he eyed Carol first, then Leonard.

"So, you two have a nice chat?" he asked gruffly. His hands clenched in a spasm of frustration and anger, and the wood cut sharply into his palms. With a low growl, he broke the bundle in half, the saguaro ribs snapping with a violent crack.

Carol jumped. Her nerves were strung so tight that *anything* could send her into a panic. She checked Cody's eyes nervously, but saw only his savage, stubborn pride.

Leonard broke the silence. "Cody, I did not come here to anger you. Please sit down." He breathed out a heavy sigh through his nostrils. "It's important, brother."

Immediately Cody was at his side. "What's wrong, Leonard? You look worried."

"It's my littlest one—"

"Annie? Your three-year-old? What's the matter?"

"She came down with that virus that's been causing sickness on the reservations. She's already running a high fever, and I am afraid of what might happen."

"The doctor in Flagstaff?"

"We have been there. He says to give her baby aspirin and wait. I cannot wait. I have been trying to get a sing organized but there have been many deaths and people are hiding in their houses. The *hatathli* will be there tomorrow night, but except for the family, nobody else is coming." He locked eyes with Cody. "I need you there with me, Cody. I need your strength, your friendship. I need your power."

"I'll be there, Leonard, and I'll use all that I know to help with the healing. You know the love that is in my heart for your family. You never have to hesitate to ask for my help. I'm only sorry that I was rude when you arrived—"

"No, do not apologize," Leonard said, giving Cody's shoulder a rough squeeze. "I understand you also."

Standing, he thanked Cody again and offered Carol his hand. "I hope to see you again. The rest of the family would like to meet you."

"And I'd like to meet them," Carol said, returning his smile, wishing there was something, anything she could do to help. She squeezed his hand. "I hope your little girl will be just fine."

As quickly as he had come, he was gone.

Carol and Cody stood looking at each other. The silence grew until it was unbearable, filled with shadows and fears too painful to admit. For what seemed like an eternity neither could speak, weighted down by the sorrow of Leonard's words. The night was dark, silent, and cold. A chill shook through Carol, making her shoulders jump and her teeth chatter.

Cody slid an arm around her and pulled her toward the fire. "Sit here, Carol. I'll bring a blanket."

After he wrapped it around her shoulders, he sat beside her, staring into the fire, his handsome face twisted with emotion. He had pulled a silver chain out of his pocket and sat rubbing a small object absent-mindedly between his fingers.

Carol squinted in the darkness, trying to discern its shape. "What is that, Cody?"

"This? An amulet. Ray and Leonard gave it to me last year. I guess they figured I needed help from whatever powers may be." He tightened his fingers around it, then sighed and slid it back into his pocket. "We will certainly need help now. The virus has plagued the desert Southwest for a year now. It can be fatal."

Carol drew in a shuddery breath. The thought of that child in danger terrified her. It tore open a tiny hole in the dam holding back her emotions, and before she could catch her breath, she was flooded with fear and grief and pain. She knew how it felt to lose a baby. . . . Oh, it mustn't happen here, not to that nice man and his family. "Can I do something?" she asked, her voice trembling.

Cody smiled at her, his ebony eyes searching deep into hers. "Don't panic yet, Lonesome. They've seen the town doctor. Now we'll have the sing—"

"That word, the one Leonard used. What does it mean?"

"*Hatathli*—well, he is a Navajo priest. First a *ndilniihii* or hand-trembler would come; he's the diagnostician. Through prayer and concentration and the use of sacred pollen, he determines where the illness lies. Once he knows what caused the sickness, he can tell the family what ceremony—"

"Sing?" Carol offered.

"Yes, 'sing' is absolutely correct." Cody nodded, his smile widening. "Then the family knows what sing the *hatathli* should perform."

Carol nodded, frowning ever so slightly. "It's fascinating, but it seems a little strange. I'm so used to doctors and specialists and technology." She leaned closer, desperately searching his face. "Maybe you should tell Leonard to take her to a hospital. Maybe you should insist—"

Cody put a finger on her lips, then brushed the hair back from her eyes with callused fingertips. "Trust me. They're going to use every means possible to help that child. They love Annie fiercely. And don't discount what you don't understand. These ceremonies have been a part of Navajo culture for centuries. They serve the People well."

Blinking back tears, she struggled to speak. "Of course. I shouldn't have said anything. I'm sorry."

Cody took her shoulders in his big hands. A comforting warmth flowed from his touch all through her body, a heat as pervasive as the heat of desire had been just an hour before. "There's nothing to apologize for. As I told you, you're far too hard on yourself, *shicho.*"

She tipped her head, liking the soft sound of the strange word. "What does that mean, Cody?"

He grinned, then shrugged, but for the first time since she'd met him, his dark eyes were clear of the pain that haunted him. "Just a Navajo term . . . a kind of endearment. I've been wanting to use it since I first saw you. It just slipped out now."

Carol leaned away, suddenly avoiding his eyes, afraid of what they might reveal. His gentleness was the one thing she wasn't prepared for. Her heart responded with an eagerness that caught her by surprise and excited her, but frightened her too. She was overreacting to everything, his words, his look, his touch. This had to stop.

Lifting her chin, Carol said softly, "Leonard did tell me about the university."

"Damn." Cody sprang to his feet and moved away, drawing the darkness around him again like a cloak. "Exactly what did he tell you?"

"What you wouldn't." Now she was looking right into his eyes, meeting their challenge. Her heart pounded but she kept her gaze steady. "He told me what you did with the artifacts. That was a pretty wild thing to do, Briggs. You had to know how the university would react."

"I did. But I had to make a choice: Put myself first, or do what I thought was right at the time. And it was my own damn fault in the first place. I trusted the wrong people. It was a costly mistake, but one I *won't* make again." He turned his back.

Carol's heart twisted. She'd reestablished the distance between them she thought she needed to have, but it felt cold away from him, cold and terribly lonely. Why, after all these years of fighting for independence, would she possibly want to depend on someone again? Trust again? Feel again? Surely she didn't. Couldn't. Wouldn't! Yet, she desperately wanted to reach out her hand and touch that broad back. . . .

Her eyes swam with tears, and her chin quivered.

But when he turned, she stood and moved away to the far side of the campfire. Her voice was filled with weariness. "I'd better get back."

"Just like that, huh?"

She blinked in the darkness. "What do you mean?"

"I mean . . ." he said, "that's some game you're playing, Lonesome."

"Me?" She gasped, amazed and annoyed.

"Yes, you." His voice cut her like a knife. "You want to tear me open, see how I work, gape at my wounds, but I'm supposed to keep my eyes closed, my mouth shut, and not react to you at all? Is that the kind of relationship you're used to?"

"I don't know what you're talking about, Cody Briggs. I was just trying to be nice. Silent as you are, I can still tell you're upset, and people say it helps to talk about your feelings. So I was only willing to listen—"

"You want to listen? Okay, I'll tell you how I feel. I feel like hell. It hurts." Cody groaned as if his pain came from a physical wound, reopened and bleeding. "I miss teaching. I miss the students, their questions, their wonder at it all. One day I was the happiest man alive, the Indiana Jones of the Southwest . . . and the next it was all gone."

His attempt at humor failed him, and he turned away, holding his head with one hand. "I loved my work. I trusted my friends. I valued their respect. I thought we shared the same ideals, passions, goals. . . . Then I found out that they didn't give a damn about any of it, not the work, not the artifacts, not me. I feel as if the world fell down around my shoulders." He paused to catch his breath, his handsome face contorted with anger and grief.

Again some uncontrollable urge took hold of Carol. She circled to him and brushed her fingertips across his clenched jaw. "I'm sorry, Cody, I am."

"I know," he said, catching hold of her hand before she could take it safely away. He pressed his lips to her palm, closed his eyes, and drew one breath. Then he released her hand and crossed his own arms over his chest. "There. I let go myself. Does that make you feel any safer?"

Carol nodded.

"Why? Tell me, Lonesome. What are you afraid of? What is there that you think you can't say?"

She shook her head violently, her hair swirling like white mist around her face. If sadness was a fog, she was lost in it. "Nothing," she whispered.

"Then this wasn't a test? 'Let's see if the man can bare his soul and survive, and if he can, maybe I can too?' That wasn't part of all this, Lonesome?"

"No. Of course not."

"Bull!"

Carol lifted her chin and glared at him. "It wasn't. Not a test, not a game—"

"Then talk to me." His hands closed around her shoulders, locking her into place between the cage of his arms. "Talk to me, Carol. I can't explain it, but we're connected in some way. In this world there are things we don't understand, powers we try to name but can't control, mysteries. And this is one of them. There's something, Carol . . . something happening between you and me. It's as though—" His grip tightened, but it was the look in his dark, mysterious eyes that made her draw a breath in a long shudder of fear. ". . . We're two halves of the same person, tied to each other, heart to heart, soul to soul. I need you to understand me so that I can make sense of what's happened. And you need the same from me."

"No!"

"Yes. Deny it all you want, but I'm inside you . . . here." One hand moved from shoulder to forehead, his fingertips resting there for a second. "And here." His fingers lifted, and settled again on the curve of her left breast, just over her heart.

Her knees gave way. One minute she was standing, trembling with fury, and the next she was sitting on the cold ground, still trembling.

"What happened?" Carol said weakly, blinking. The whole world seemed to jump and flicker like the firelight.

Cody gently tightened his hands on her shoulders. He was kneeling in front of her, his face just inches from hers. His eyes were luminous, as deep and dark as the night sky, but they burned now with a tenderness she couldn't escape.

A hiccup of choked grief rose to her throat. She ducked her head and slid away, turning within the confines of his grasp. "It doesn't matter; I'm fine now. You can let go."

"What if I don't want to?" he asked softly, still as gentle as a man could be.

"Do it anyway. Because I say so." She swung her head back to stare at him, the pupils of her eyes crowding out the blue. Her hands shook.

He held her still. "Then will you trust me?"

Carol flinched, his words thrusting into her heart like an arrow, perfectly on target. But she was quickly regaining her self-control. "Not necessarily. Besides, there's nothing I need to trust you with. As I said, I'm perfectly fine now."

"Good," he answered, a small smile playing across his beautifully chiseled mouth. "You look perfectly fine. Delicious, as a matter of fact. The fire lights your hair like a halo around your face. Maybe what you really are is an angel, come down to save me."

She gave a weak little laugh and shook her head. "Unlikely, Cody. If that's what you think, then you really *are* a terrible judge of character." She gathered her feet under her and stood suddenly, brushing the sand off her bottom and hips. She was scowling, pale brows furrowed, mouth pursed. But when she stopped fussing long enough to look at him, her breath stopped in her chest.

He was sitting there, arms wrapped around his knees, bare chest burnished by firelight, grinning up at her. The vulnerability was gone, and he looked dangerous again . . . predatory. For an instant she was absolutely mesmerized by the tantalizing grace and beauty of his big body. Every line of flesh and muscle was perfectly sculpted, teasingly real. Raw power lurked just beneath the shining veneer of that bronzed skin, an animal heat and strength leashed by his fierce will. And something glinted in his eyes, lusty and untamed, revealed for an instant like a wink.

Carol gasped. When she found her voice, it came out in a squeak. "What are you doing, Cody Briggs?"

"Me? Just watching you."

"Don't. Get up and take me back to the hotel."

"I *don't* think so," he replied, teeth flashing white in the darkness.

"What do you mean, 'you don't think so'? How else am I going to get back?"

"The same way you got here, I guess. I hadn't given it any thought."

"Well, start thinking about it." She paced away around the fire, glaring at him. She needed some distance between them if she was going to work up some righteous anger. "Cody, it's *your* Jeep that broke down."

"Mesa Tours' Jeep. I only drive it."

"Don't be cute, Briggs."

"Can't help myself, Lawson."

Carol stormed back and stood in front of him, hands on hips. "Cody, you have to go with me and fix the Jeep. I have to be at work in the morning."

"In the morning I'll fix it."

"Fix it now," she demanded, her voice snapping like the flames. "I mean it! Get up now . . . please."

"Ah, that's nicer. At least I'll get up." The muscles tightened in his legs, his shoulders, his back as he stood, and then he was towering above her, his bare chest inches from her face. He smelled of wood smoke and sage, the cool night, the warm scent of a man. Her eyelids fluttered.

"Are you going to faint on me again?"

"Absolutely not!" she snapped. "I didn't faint the first time. Just got a little dizzy, that's all. I'm just tired. I don't sleep well."

"Why not?" Knowing she wouldn't answer, he stormed on. "You work too hard. And you probably don't eat. Did you even have dinner before you came out here?"

"Yes, of course," she said, thinking there must have been a sandwich back there somewhere in the not-too-distant past. She couldn't seem to remember. "Cody . . . go fix the Jeep."

"Carol, it's dark and it's cold out there now."

"Well, put on a shirt, for God's sake!" That would make her life simpler immediately. And if she could only be back in her safe little room, maybe she would get some sleep tonight. She hadn't felt so tired, so utterly exhausted in years. Reaching up, she took hold of his upper arms, her fingers digging into his flesh. "Cody, you have to!"

Her touch seared him like a brand, making him hers forever. He felt it through flesh and bone, right down to his wounded soul. His muscles tightened, fired by the bitter habit of anger and withdrawal, but he held himself stock-still, waiting, watching. His body trembled with latent emotion, suddenly caged. And over it all washed the heat of passion. He'd been fantasizing her touch all afternoon, dreaming what it would be like to have her touch him, stroke him, hold him. Now it had happened, and his body was already driving on to the inevitable conclusion.

Inhaling sharply, he drew his head back. Stunned by the power of the lust raging through him, he glared down at her, his body stiff and motionless. Her small hands were still wrapped around his biceps, nails digging into the muscles. They looked like two small animals clinging to a hard cliff wall. He almost had to smile. The urge made a tic jump at the corner of his mouth, and his eyes softened. "I don't have to do anything, Carol."

"You do!" she cried, frantic with confusion. She

should let go, but she *couldn't* let go. He felt so big and strong. So wonderfully strong that all her fears and sorrows felt suddenly smaller and less lethal. This man could protect her, save her, love her. This man could be a place to hide, a place to stop and to start again, a place to be happy. She had to let go of him, put an end to this ridiculous, embarrassing little scene, but she couldn't. When she did, she'd be back to reality, alone and lost. *Oh dear God, please . . . help me.*

She felt him shift beneath her hands, his skin sliding beneath her palms, his arms pulling out from under her touch, and then she was being lifted, held against his hard, naked chest, crushed against the heat and power of his body. She felt his rippling muscles, coiled with a tense, primitive passion; heat rose from his skin, spiced with his musky male scent. Her senses reeled. Against her belly she felt the long, hard urgency of his arousal.

She gasped, and Cody responded by plunging his tongue into the sweet, honeyed cave of her mouth. Her breath was warm on his mouth; he drank it down into his lungs and felt its heady liquor swirl to hot flame in his belly and loins. As much as he'd fantasized this moment, spent the entire afternoon in a repressed erotic daze, nothing had prepared him for the luscious feel of her body pressed against his. He had to hold her, touch her, taste her.

A sudden pool of wetness formed in the hot secret place between Carol's legs. She was melting, gone soft as butter in the sun. Her breasts felt swollen, her nipples beading into tender little points of exquisite sensitivity. She'd never felt such excitement, or such animal longing. She wanted to rub against his body like a cat, her back arched, her fur all electric with pure sexuality. This couldn't be her; this *mustn't* be her.

Her faint struggles in his arms brought her belly rubbing back and forth against his hard, aching sex. Cody groaned, a sound torn from deep within his chest. His hands tightened around the fragile cage of her ribs; he could feel the breath squeeze out of her.

How could someone so small and vulnerable have such total power over him? Carefully he eased his hold, letting her slim warmth slide down his body. He felt her feet touch ground, and he groaned again, missing the sweet weight of her in his arms. "Carol, you're killing me," he whispered to the crown of her head, his lips pressed into the warm silk of her hair. Fine as a baby's hair, he thought, warning himself: *you've gotta be gentle. Be slow and gentle with this girl, Briggs. She's been hurt . . . terribly hurt. Be gentle.*

But his body was like a wild mustang fighting at the end of the reins. And if she didn't stop wiggling against him, he was going to explode. He'd have to take her, love her, slide into the silken heat of her and make her want him as much as he wanted her. "Lonesome," he said with a growl, needing to lick dry lips to even speak. "Lord in Heaven, Lonesome, stop that wriggling or I'm going to do what I want to do instead of what I *should* do."

Carol went absolutely still, top to toe. "And what

is that?" she squeaked, looking up at him with wide
stunned eyes.

Cody laughed, a rough, sexy sound that rumbled
through his broad chest. "You know damn well what I
mean."

Slowly the night took shape and texture around
her. There were stars twinkling in the sky, the fire
crackling at her back, a hard, warm body in her arms.
"I guess I do," she whispered, leaning her forehead
against his bare chest. The smell of him filled her
senses; she was still wet and aching. She shook her
head in helpless confusion.

Cody frowned down at her. "It's all right. Whatever it is, I'll make it all right."

Carol reacted as if she'd been stung. Her whole
body tightened. "You can't," she cried. "You don't
understand—"

"Then tell me, dammit. I care about you. I want
to hold you, help you—"

"No! I'm not ready. Way back, almost nine years
back, I did trust someone. I was young and silly. I
trusted him, and something terrible happened—"

"What?" Cody demanded, wrapping his arms
tighter around her; she was trembling like a reed in
the wind.

"No . . . no . . ." she whispered, steeling herself against his touch. "This is all happening too
quickly. Stop. Let me go."

Cody took a half step back. He looked down at
her, his eyes fierce with pain and passion. "I can let

you go for now, Lonesome, but I don't know if I can stop. I want to help you, not hurt you."

Carol shook her head, mute with grief. In the firelight her tears left silver tracks on her pale, pale skin. She bit her lips, looked away, wiped her face on her sleeve. "Now look what you've done, Briggs, darn you."

"I didn't do anything, Lonesome," he answered in a low, ragged voice. "Someone else did. And I'm sorry. I'd kill the bastard if I could. I'd rescue you before it ever happened. I'd—"

"Stop it! I'm not listening, Briggs. You're just making it worse." She sniffed mightily and used the other sleeve. Damn, he didn't even have a shirt on. She was embarrassed. His chest was wet from her tears. And what was that mascara on his glistening skin? Cocking an elbow, she squeezed an arm in between them and scrubbed at his chest.

"Forget that, Lonesome, it's okay—"

"It's not!" Stepping back, she glared up at him, tears clinging to her lashes. "I'm embarrassed. This isn't me. It's not!" she cried. "I told you I'm tired. Maybe I'm coming down with the flu or something. But this doesn't have anything to do with you, and that's for damn sure."

He had to stifle the urge to throttle her. Instead he gritted his teeth. "Fine. I believe you."

"Good. Now if you'd go fix the lousy Jeep, I'll be on my way."

Cody stiffened and strode away. She saw him bend for something, and when he turned back he was shrugging into a shirt, his beautiful body disappearing into the dark folds of the fabric. But then his hands fell away from the buttons, as if even that task was too difficult. He shook his head, hair swinging across cheek and jaw like the slash of a dark knife. "I'm going to make that cup of coffee now. You want some?"

"No." She turned to face the fire. The night had gotten colder, and she felt weak enough to believe she really had caught some bug. If he didn't fix the Jeep, what would she do? Walk back to the hotel? Sagging under the hopelessness of her situation, she felt the threat of tears rise again. She needed to be alone, to nurse her aching heart, still her confusion. She needed to curl up in the corner of the couch where she could feel safe, watch late-night TV, and not think or feel. Maybe she *would* walk.

There was a rustle of sound behind her. Then nothing. Carol peeked over her shoulder, and there was Cody, sitting on the edge of a sleeping bag just a few feet away. His powerful muscles bunched beneath the thin cotton of his shirt, and his chest gleamed in the firelight. Sitting cross-legged like that, his thighs strained at the denim of his jeans. But it was his eyes, black as the night and just as impenetrable, that shattered the little calm she had. "You're not going to help me, are you?"

"I would if you'd let me, Lonesome," he said softly.

"Darn it, Briggs, you know what I mean."

"The answer to that is no. I'm not going out into the desert in the middle of the night to repair a car. I couldn't if I wanted to. Hell, I couldn't see well enough to change a tire, let alone fix whatever you broke. But—" He ignored her irate response. "But I will go out at first light. Before I head up to Leonard's, I'll make sure you're back at the hotel in time to put on your perfect makeup, your perfect clothes, and be behind your nice, safe desk with time to spare. Okay?"

Her two-word response was short and to the point.

Cody just threw back his head and laughed. "Didn't know they said stuff like that back in the heart o' Dixie, Lonesome. But if you're suddenly willing—"

"I'd chew cactus thorns first," she snapped, trying desperately to hold on to her anger. "So where am I going to sleep?"

"Right here," he said, patting the sleeping bag. "It's a good bag, plenty warm for a night like this. I've used it up in the Superstition Mountains in a foot of snow and—"

"I don't want a rundown on your camping adventures, Cody Briggs. Where are *you* going to sleep?"

The grin Cody had been fighting got away from him. "Right in here with you, Lonesome. I promise to behave."

"Think again, cowboy."

His deep, warm laughter rolled across the desert once more. Kicking off his boots, unthreading his belt, he slipped back out of his shirt and into the sleeping bag. He held the edge open for her. "Come on. I won't bite."

Carol thought for a moment, but there really seemed to be no alternatives. She was growing colder by the minute. And *suddenly* that sleeping bag with that big dark, strong chest to snuggle against seemed like the most inviting thing she'd ever seen.

It didn't make any sense, but she'd gone beyond sense to some strange world she couldn't understand but desired. Reality had been so confusing for so long . . . this couldn't be any worse. Maybe she'd even get some sleep.

"Don't think I like this," she warned.

"Oh, I don't."

"Don't think I'm doing it willingly. I haven't got any choice, thanks to you."

"I'm well aware that it's all my fault." He nodded, black eyes flashing.

"And don't you try anything, or I'll borrow that knife of yours and take the wild out of your wild West."

"Woman, you've worn me out. I feel as if I just fought at the Little Big Horn on the losing side. Get in here, if you're coming. I'm going to sleep."

"Move over. Farther," she said, lining her tennis shoes up neatly next to the sleeping bag. Gingerly she slid her jean-clad legs down into the bag, then her hips, then her torso. But no matter how careful she was, she couldn't help but brush against his big, hard body. "Can't you move over more?"

"Carol," he said, and growled, fighting his own

silent war. "This is a one-man bag, and I'm one good-size man. You're on borrowed space. Just lay down and lay still, for God's sake."

"I am." She curled onto her side and tried to relax. But just trying to find a comfortable place for her head had her twisting and turning.

Cody groaned. Her corn-silk hair was brushing his cheek, his lips, his chin. The scent of her filled his nostrils, trailed down his throat, and filled his lungs like some intoxicating incense. He wanted to push his whole face into her skin, run his tongue across that silken sweetness and taste her, smell her, touch every inch of her. This time his groan started deep in his gut.

"Stop making that noise, Briggs. You sound like some dangerous animal."

"I am a dangerous animal." He growled. "Here. Rest your head on my arm, and then lie still." Without waiting for her to obey, he rolled onto his side, then reached across her with his free arm and yanked the zipper up around them. Leaning back, his bicep grazed the soft, sensitive side of her breast.

Carol gasped. The heat of him behind her was nothing like the heat of the campfire. This was potently alive, potently male. As if in self-defense, her skin went cold as ice.

"You okay?"

"Fine," she whispered, shivering uncontrollably.

"Then why are you shaking like that, Lonesome? Can I help?"

"No. It just happens sometimes."

"Well, it *shouldn't* happen. Don't you know that? A beautiful, tender, capable, lovely woman like you, you shouldn't be shaking in the dark. You should be happy. Carefree. Bold as brass."

"Life doesn't always work the way it should, Cody," she whispered, unbidden tears rising.

"Maybe not in the past, Lonesome . . . but the future's not written yet. There's hope. Right?" He nudged his chin into the nape of her neck and wrapped his free arm around her, snuggling her back against him, into the cradle of his chest and hips. When she started to struggle, he whispered in her ear. "Shhhh. . . . It's all right, sweet thing. We're just gonna sleep now. Close your eyes. Breathe deep. What are you going to dream about?"

"Nothing!" she said quickly, sniffing. "I *hope*. I'd like one night without dreams."

"Okay, then that's what you'll get."

She gave a little snicker of laughter; impolite as it was, she just couldn't help herself. "You make that sound like a guarantee. My therapist wasn't able to accomplish that miracle in three years. What have you got? Magic?"

"Maybe." His voice was a low, husky drawl, strangely bewitching in the dark.

The shaking had stopped. Carol tensed, listening to her body, waiting for her nighttime devils to return. But instead she felt the heat and strength of that big body at her back.

Cody held her lightly, reining in the fierce desire that flooded his loins. He would lie still and let her sleep. He would, even if it killed him.

In his arms, Carol felt like a tightly coiled spring, so tense, it made *his* muscles ache in sympathy. And he did understand that fear, that wariness. Sharing sleep with someone was an incredible act of trust; it left you defenseless, open, and vulnerable. Sleep hadn't been his friend either this last year, but it was nothing like the panic he sensed in her. Now, finally, that terrible shivering had passed. Her skin was growing warm, and her breathing was reaching an even, slow rhythm.

Slowly, minute by minute, he felt her unwind and relax. Then she stirred, and her tight little rear brushed against his groin. He had to count backward from one hundred to keep from groaning aloud.

Then, just when he thought she was almost asleep, she lifted her head and looked sleepily back at him over her shoulder. "You know what Leonard told me? He says you've got the love wink."

Cody laughed softly in surprise. "What?"

"Never mind . . ." she whispered, mumbling to herself. "Maybe this *is* all a dream."

"No dreams . . ." he whispered. "No dreams, I promise. . . ." But he was talking only to himself. This was no dream. Ready or not, whether he liked it or not. Laying there, holding her in his arms, he felt his shattered soul begin to mend. It scared the hell out of him. Silently, from the beginning, he said a chant that Leonard taught him that was supposed to give a person the inner strength to deal with difficult situations. He said it for himself, and then he said it again for everyone struggling for happiness under that darkened sky.

EIGHT

"You don't need to be afraid of me, Lonesome," Cody said softly, though she had barely stirred. "That I swear. And I don't make idle threats, nor idle promises."

Carol opened her eyes to the first pink light of dawn. She was alone in the sleeping bag. Cody had lit the fire and now he was hunkered down near the little camp stove, spooning coffee grounds into an old tin pot.

"I believe that much," she whispered.

He had been watching her, waiting for her answer, and now he nodded and looked back at his work.

Carol snuggled back into the bag, pulling the flannel edge up to her chin. She ached for the heat of him there beside her. And then she realized something. "I didn't have any bad dreams last night," she exclaimed in amazement.

"I know. You slept so soundly, I had to lean over

and check your pulse a couple of times." Despite his bantering tone, Cody was remembering the sweet heaviness of her head on his arm, the way her bones had seemed to melt in sleep as she curled against his chest and belly. Heat circled his loins at the memory. Nestled together like spoons, he had felt the breath move in and out of her lungs, had felt the soft beat of her heart. It was as if their bodies were one, joined. He'd never known such absolute intimacy before, and it left a wild emptiness in his chest, part excitement and part fear.

Something else had happened that he could not forget. She *had* begun to dream, her breathing growing fast and shallow, her eyelids fluttering. He had wrapped her in his arms and held her close until she stilled and fell back into the deepest sleep. It had happened twice, and both times he felt a strange, sharp grief cut through him. He'd clenched his teeth, muscles tensed against the pain, and used what power he had to draw it away from her, taking it into himself. Now he smiled to himself. She remembered only sleep. No bad dreams.

"What's so funny, Briggs? I didn't snore or anything, did I?" Carol demanded.

"Nope." He slid her a glance from under his dark lashes. "But I'll keep an ear open next time."

"Ha! In your dreams." She felt surprisingly relaxed and playful. And aroused. His nearness had her aching with an unfamiliar yearning. She wanted it to be night again. But a tiny worry nagged at her subconscious. "I didn't say anything in my sleep, did I?"

"What are you so worried about, Lonesome? You were fine. What deep, dark secrets do you think you let slip?"

Carol gave him an icy laugh. "Prototype design for the new Stealth bomber."

One dark brow rose. "Interesting you named a weapon. What's the matter? Afraid whatever it is, I'm going to use it against you?"

All Carol's newly discovered peace deserted her. Her heart slammed against her ribs and suddenly she was cold with sweat. "Trust me, Briggs, I don't give you even a second thought—"

"Trust *me*, *shicho*, because you can. You don't have to be pissed at me. I won't hurt you."

Her breath stopped in her throat. Damn this man. For nine years she'd kept everything safely locked away, and now this man . . . *this* man—Maybe he *was* magic. Even though he'd turned away, reaching for the coffeepot, she could feel him touching her, holding her.

"Have a cup of coffee, Lonesome. You look like you need it."

"I always need a cup of coffee in the morning. *All* civilized people do." Carol sat up, shaking her hair loose, then using her fingers to comb it back into shape. Sipping at the hot liquid, she coughed, pressed a hand to her chest, then peered cautiously into the mug. "Whew! Cody, this stuff is strong enough to put hair on your chest."

"Oh, I certainly hope not, Carol." He gave a snort

of laughter, breaking the tension. "Sorry. Guess I've gotten used to doing things to suit myself out here."

"Well . . ." She shrugged, tossing the coffee into the sand. "Go fix the Jeep, and I'll be out of your hair. You can be back to having things just how you like them."

"I didn't say I like them. I just said I'd gotten used to them."

"It's the same thing." Carol sighed loudly, feeling her sadness settle around her for the day. "One's as good as the other."

Cody set the pot down, dusted his hands on his knees, and stood. There was a sharp crease in his brow as he stared down at her. "Even you don't believe that, Lonesome."

"Ooh, I hate when you do that!" she snapped. Yanking at the zipper of the sleeping bag, she struggled to get out of it but succeeded only in snagging it on the lining. "Darn and double darn," she swore, adding some colorful Southern imprecations. "Get me out of this thing, Briggs."

In seeming obedience, Cody knelt down and reached for the zipper. It took Carol a second to realize he and the sleeping bag were scrunched into this little space right between his legs. Her gaze lifted from that inverted *V* of denim, over his fly, his belt, his chest, his throat, and locked with his black and glinting eyes.

She blushed, her hot cheeks fanned by the cool morning air. "And what do you think you're doing?"

"Helping you. You're stuck, Carol, stuck inside. I'm offering you a way out."

Carol swallowed; her throat was hot and dry. Revved by anger, she wriggled her way right out of the bag *and* his reach. "There. Did it myself!" Hurrying across the clearing, she grabbed his shirt and threw it at him.

Cody caught it one-handed, but he continued to kneel over the flattened cocoon of the sleeping bag, the same brash grin lighting his face.

"What now, Briggs?" Carol felt if he looked at her like that for one more second, she was going to explode, or suffer meltdown, *some* awful thing from which she'd never be the same. And *he* looked different.

There in the pearly light of dawn, backlit by the fire, his outline suddenly blurred and shifted. For a moment it was as if she were seeing again the double image of something bigger and wilder around him. Some power, or energy or force? Her brain grasped at names and explanations. Her heart raced. Who was this man? What was his magic?

She blinked and swallowed. "Cody?"

He shuddered, then swept his fingers through his hair. "Lonesome—"

"What?" she whispered, dreading the answer, yet wishing it would be something she could share, some astonishing thing that would solve all her problems.

"Never mind." He shook his head, shrugged into his shirt. The material hung down from his broad shoulders, barely covering the plates of muscle on his chest. His stomach was washboard ridged. But he seemed totally unaware of himself, as if for the moment he didn't even inhabit his fabulous body. When he glanced up, his dark gaze sweeping the sky, Carol's eyes followed.

She stood transfixed for a moment, seeing only a small black dot soaring cloud high but feeling shivers walk along her skin. An eagle.

Grabbing her purse, she hurried to the edge of the campsite. "I'm going, Cody. Are you coming?"

He seemed to materialize at her shoulder, and overtook her in two strides. "You bet. We've both got to get going."

She glanced at him. "Are you driving this morning?"

"No. Not today or tomorrow. Good thing, because I've got to head up to Leonard's soon to prepare for the sing. I've got to hurry." He still seemed distracted, his thoughts elsewhere. "And then if everything's okay, tomorrow I've got an appointment over at Apache tribal headquarters to determine the authenticity of some artifacts they've unearthed along the Salt River Canyon. Now that's a pretty place. I'll have to take you sometime."

"I don't think so." Carol put a hand on his hard, muscled shoulder, focusing his concentration. No matter how difficult he made this, she was determined to be honest, to explain as much as she dared. And he had to listen. "Cody, I don't want to lead you on. I'm not ready for this. I want to slow it down. I need time and space for myself. Are you listening to me? I don't want you to get the wrong idea."

"But what if it's the right idea, *shicho?*" His deep voice sent chills running up and down her arms. He'd halted in front of her, blocking the path, and now all his fierce concentration was focused directly on her.

Mustering her courage, she met his gaze. "It's not, Cody. That's what I'm trying to tell you." He could see right into her, her confusion, her turmoil . . . and all the while his eyes revealed his own brutally honest emotions.

"Cody, please listen to me. I'm serious. I have stuff I have to work out—"

"What 'stuff,' Lonesome? Tell me. I can't stand it when you look that way—"

"It's not your problem, Briggs."

"Then whose is it?"

"Mine," she cried, her self-control shattering. "Just mine alone."

"But who's going to share it with you? You need to let someone in—"

She shook her head violently. "No! I can't. I *won't.* I told you, I made the mistake once of trusting someone, but I learned from it. I'm careful now. I can take care of myself. I don't need anyone else."

"Wrong. You're so wrong. What are you going to do? Carry that sorrow around all by yourself until it wears you down past where you can hope or dream or feel anything but sadness? Carol—" He tried to take her in his arms and hold her, protect her, offer her his own body to lean against, but she pushed him away.

"Don't, Cody!"

"You are your own worst enemy." He swore, his voice rough with emotion. "Let me in. Let me help, even if it's just as a friend—"

"I don't *need* a friend. I need a Jeep, and a way back to the hotel. That's *all* I need. Then I can get to work and be myself."

"Be *by* yourself, you mean."

"Don't start telling me what I mean. I know what I mean. And what I want. I'm fine the way I am. I'm busy and I'm happy—"

"Being busy is *not* the same as being happy, Lonesome. What in God's name happened to make you forget that?" Without thinking, he seized her narrow shoulders and pulled her tightly against his chest, wanting desperately to hold her, comfort her, kiss away those tears.

But she hit at him, her small fists finding mostly air, but landing with occasional soft thumps against his hands and arms and chest. "Shut up, Cody. Just shut up! Leave me alone. I mean it. If you say one more word, just one more, I will never speak to you again. And I don't make idle threats or promises, either!"

They hadn't spoken while he fixed the oil pan on the Jeep, a patch job that lasted only for the short ride back to the hotel. Confusion, fear, and pain churned through her, until she tasted bitterness in her throat and was afraid she was going to be sick.

Helping her out of the Jeep, Cody pulled her against him, capturing her there for just a moment. He held her, and she was too afraid of making a scene to do more than struggle feebly within his arms, not making a sound. His voice was muffled, his face pressed into her pale windblown hair, but she heard each word as if it was burnt into her brain. "I'll try to stay away, Lonesome . . . if that's what you really want."

"Yes," she said into the soft denim of his shirt. "Yes. It is."

Without another word he spun and strode away, only pausing to shout back over his shoulder, "Tell Mesa Tours to come fetch their damn Jeep."

Carol felt released and abandoned, all at the same time. Waves of emotion swept over her. She longed to call him back, to say his name and have him there beside her. She ached to lose herself in the passion he awoke, to blaze and burn without thought or care. But she couldn't. She mustn't. He'd overwhelm her in an instant, consume her, reduce her caution to ashes.

No.

This was her life, and she intended to live it carefully, sensibly, safely. Only she knew the cost of the terrible mistake she'd made nine years earlier. Only she paid that cost, day after day, year after year. And only she could make the right, the necessary decisions. Her life was improving. She was successful, competent, earning a decent living, able to take care of herself no matter what happened. No matter what. . . .

Get swept away...

Enter the

Dream Come True Sweepstakes

You could win a romantic rendezvous in diamond-blue Hawaii...the gothic splendor of Europe...or the sun-drenched Caribbean. To enter, make your choice with one of these tickets. If you win, you'll be swept away to your dream destination!

Get 4 FREE Loveswept Romances!

or take $20,000 Cash!

 Whisk me to Hawaii

 Carry Me Off To Europe

 Take me to the Caribbean

 Pamper me with FREE GIFTS!

GET A FREE GIFT!

Get this personal, lighted makeup case. It's yours absolutely FREE!

NO OBLIGATION TO BUY.
See details inside...

Get Swept Away To Your Romantic Holiday!

Imagine being wrapped in the embrace of your lover's arms, watching glorious Hawaiian rainbows born only for you. Imagine strolling through the gothic haunts of romantic London. Imagine being drenched in the sun-soaked beauty of the Caribbean. If you crave such journeys then enter now to...

WIN A ROMANTIC RENDEZVOUS!
Or Take $20,000 CASH!

Seize the moment and enter to win one of these exotic rendezvous vacations. To enter affix the destination ticket of your choice to the Official Entry Form and drop it in the mail. It costs you absolutely nothing to enter—not even postage! So take a chance on romance and enter today!

Loveswept®

Has More In Store For You With
4 FREE BOOKS and a FREE GIFT!

We've got four FREE Loveswept Romances and a FREE Lighted Makeup Case ready to send you.

Place the FREE GIFTS ticket on your Entry Form, and your first shipment of Loveswept Romances is yours absolutely FREE—*and that means no shipping and handling charges.*

Plus, about once a month, you'll get four *new* books hot off the presses, *before they're in the bookstores*, and, from time to time, special editions of select *Loveswept* Romances. You'll always have 15 days to decide whether to keep any shipment, for our low regular price, currently just $2.50 per book.* **You are never obligated to keep any shipment**, and you may cancel at any time by writing "cancel" across our invoice and returning the shipment to us, at our expense. There's **no risk** and **no obligation** to buy, *ever.*

It's a pretty seductive offer, we've made even more attractive with the **Lighted Makeup Case—yours absolutely FREE!** It's a lovely piece including an assortment of brushes for eye shadow, blush and lip color. And with the lighted makeup mirror *you* can make sure he'll always see the passion in your eyes!

BOTH GIFTS ARE ABSOLUTELY FREE AND ARE YOURS TO KEEP FOREVER, no matter what you decide about future shipments! So come on! You risk nothing at all—and you stand to gain a world of sizzling romance, exciting prizes…and FREE GIFTS!

* (plus shipping & handling, and sales tax in NY, and GST in Canada. Prices slightly higher in Canada.)

ENTER NOW FOR A CHANCE TO WIN A ROMANTIC RENDEZVOUS!

or take $20,000 Cash!

No risk and no obligation to buy, anything, *ever!*

Dream Come True

SWEEPSTAKES
OFFICIAL ENTRY FORM

☐ **YES!** Enter me in the sweepstakes! I've affixed the destination ticket for the Romantic Rendezvous of my choice to this Entry Form. I've also affixed the FREE GIFTS ticket. So please, send me my 4 FREE BOOKS and FREE Lighted Makeup Case.

Affix Destination Ticket of Your Choice Here	TICKET	Affix FREE GIFTS Ticket Here	

PLEASE PRINT CLEARLY   4B103   20826

NAME

ADDRESS

CITY   APT. #

STATE   ZIP

☐ **NO**, I don't want to take advantage of your risk-free offer, but enter me in the Dream Come True Sweepstakes anyway. I have affixed my destination ticket above.

There is no purchase necessary to enter the sweepstakes. To enter without taking advantage of the risk-free offer, return the entry form with only the romantic destination ticket affixed. To be eligible, sweepstakes entries must be received by the deadline found in the accompanying rules at the back of the book. There is no obligation to buy when you send for your free books and free lighted makeup case. You may preview each new shipment for 15 days risk-free. If you decide against it, simply return the shipment within 15 days and owe nothing. If you keep them, pay our low regular price, currently just $2.50 each book—a savings of $1.00 per book off the cover price (plus shipping & handling, and sales tax in NY, and GST in Canada. Prices slightly higher in Canada.)

Prices subject to change. Orders subject to approval. See complete sweepstakes rules at the back of the book.

Don't miss your chance to win a romantic rendezvous and get 4 FREE BOOKS and a FREE Lighted Makeup Case!

You risk nothing—so enter now!

Again the sadness washed through her. Then she'd been helpless, vulnerable, unable to take care of herself, let alone that tiny, brand-new life. The tears rose, hot and fresh as on that earlier day. But everything had changed. She wasn't that foolish, innocent girl. She was a sensible, clear-eyed woman.

Squaring her shoulders, she glanced around to assure herself that no one had been witness to her confusion, dusted off her jeans, and hurried around the corner of the hotel to her own little room in the employee's quarters. A shower. A toothbrush. Fresh clothes. Work. That was enough.

Sitting behind the concierge desk at nine A.M. on the dot, Carol felt safe and back in control. She clung to that security all morning, not stopping to eat or think. And at noon, when everyone else was hurrying here or there for lunch, Carol stayed where she was, trying to work on her operations manual. But, for the first time, work didn't provide the haven her soul was seeking. Her head was filled with thoughts of Cody, and Leonard, and babies crying . . . the present and the past all whirling together.

Carol frowned and rubbed at her temples with her fingertips. Not only did her head ache, but her neck and shoulders were tight as springs. She felt like a jack-in-the-box, pushed into too small a space, ready to pop its top. And then, once again, she thought of Leonard and Ray, and how *they* must feel, their worry and fear and sadness, and about the approaching ceremonial. Oh, that poor little child! If only there was something she could do, some way she could help. . . .

At least she'd try.

Luckily Edna Yazzie was still at her desk.

"Edna, do you happen to know Leonard John?"

"Sure. He's married to my cousin Ray. They don't live too far from where I live. As a matter of fact, I'm going there this afternoon for a sing. His little girl is ill."

"I know. I met him last night with Cody Briggs, and he told me all about it. Edna, is there something I can do? I can't seem to get a bit of work done today; all I seem to be able to think about is their little girl. Maybe there's errands I could run, or medicine I could pick up, or something. I don't know—" Carol stopped, watching the other woman's broad face, fearing she'd overstepped some line of propriety she wasn't even aware of. She shrugged and slipped her hands into her skirt pockets.

"Do you want to come?"

"Pardon me?" Carol said, straightening up.

"Do you want to come to the sing? As a stranger, you might have to sit outside, not in the hogan but nearby."

"Oh, I don't want to intrude," Carol said quickly, trying to hide her eagerness. Suddenly she felt this was right. She had to be there. She was *supposed* to be there. But she asked again, "Are you sure I wouldn't be intruding?"

Edna looked right into her eyes. "I see how much

you care. That's a very strong thing, that kind of compassion. I think maybe you should be there." She nodded, paused as if listening to an inner voice, then nodded again. "The more people sending up their prayers, the more power for healing and harmony. Yes. We'll leave at three."

NINE

Edna dropped Carol off near Leonard's homestead. A pretty creek ran through it, east to west. There was the hogan, the traditional six-sided, dome-roofed Navajo home, a corral down near the willows lining the creek, and a small garden still studded with dried stalks of corn and beans. But she was drawn to a smaller structure that sat off by itself, smoke rising from the roof hole, looking to her like prayers made visible as the participants purified themselves for the healing ceremony. That was the sweat lodge.

Carol didn't dare approach. Everyone was busy preparing for the sing; even Edna had disappeared. There was no one to tell her where she should sit, what she should do, and she certainly didn't want to offend. But more and more strongly she felt that she had to be somewhere nearby. It was as if her heart had been led there.

A few jumbled rocks sat under a lone tree near the

far corner of the corral. They formed a little bench just made for sitting . . . so she sat, and waited.

In moments the men emerged from the sweat lodge, bare-chested and bare-legged, glistening and chanting, moving in the slow ritualized movements of a dream state. They would proceed from the sweat to the hogan where the curing ceremonial would take place. Already there was the sound of drums and rattles; the sand painting was completed; the chanting had begun. Now the people would join together and use everything they had, their voices, prayers, strength, symbols and love, to put themselves in touch with the power of eternal forces and bring the child back to the "path of beauty."

A heavy mist had risen and was drifting through the willows and over the creek, hiding Carol from notice, though not a single person seemed to be aware of her presence. She felt as if she were cloaked in a magical invisibility that hid her from sight, yet seemed oddly to sharpen her own perceptions. Now . . . right now . . . all she saw was Cody Briggs.

He was taller than the Navajos surrounding him, tall and gleaming, but his face wore the same mystical expression of intensity and power. He was the most beautiful man Carol had ever seen, and half naked as he was, he sent goose bumps climbing over her skin. There was a secret, sensual pleasure to spying on him like this, as though she'd wandered into a hidden world of might and majesty, of unknown power, of myth and legend. That's what the mists revealed: A man who was heroic, magical, astonishing.

Roused by the drumbeats, her desire surged through unexpected channels. A trickle of sweat ran down between her breasts. Her mouth was dry with desire. At the top of her thighs, her pulse beat like the drum sounding low and mysterious through the valley. If *she* were magic, there were things she'd do. She'd cast a spell on him and bring him to her, lay him down in the heat and the dust, and run her hands over his body. She'd untie the thong around his waist and know what was hidden there. She would use her mouth, her tongue, her fingertips, her nipples, and discover what she'd been missing all these long years.

Suddenly, for the first time, she wanted her life to be different than it was. She wanted to be excited, to be in love, to be daring again. She wanted some of this magic for herself. Her life felt dry as dust to her, dull and deadly. Her own body felt as if it had to belong to someone else, it was so boring, so disappointing. But there was a flicker of life there between her legs, a hot reminder of what she could be, should be feeling. She flicked her tongue over dry lips, staring at his broad, bronzed back. Three more steps and he'd vanish into the hogan . . . two . . . one . . . Wild dark hair, muscled shoulders, lean flanks . . . she couldn't bear to lose sight of him. She stared harder. *Turn* . . .

Cody turned as if he'd heard the wind call his name. His eyes, dark and blazing with the golden lights of the ceremonial fire, scanned the surroundings in puzzlement, searching for the unexpected— and found it. Was she really there, a flicker of pale gold flame in the mist, or was this part of the vision that had overtaken him so fiercely in the sweat lodge? His senses whirled and shifted like the smoke in the sacred darkness; his blood thrummed in his veins with the fierce wildness of the drums that sounded suddenly like huge wings beating in the air. His gaze locked on hers. And in his chest something woke and soared, a wild and predatory creature, eagle-eyed, eagle-fierce, that swooped through time and distance to seize this woman for its own.

Carol reeled with shock. She'd felt it, a tightening around her heart as if sharp talons had locked themselves in her tender flesh and were pulling her closer, tugging at her heart, lifting her out of herself. She couldn't think; the air was loud with the beat of huge wings. There was heat and noise and fear and ecstasy. Here was everything she feared . . . and wanted. Her body was driven by the longing to yield, to soar, to fly, to leap without thought, to abandon caution and sanity, to escape finally from all that hurt her. Oh, to be happy! To be loved and desired and sated with pleasure and to give that in return. Could she? Dare she?

Between them, the air shimmered and shifted with magic. Later she would try to explain it, but now the magic held sway. It filled the mist with its own huge but benevolent power, love beyond thought or reason, beyond the realm of the ordinary.

The drums rose, calling.

The sweat on Cody's chest was licked by the wind; the bones in his arms ached as if they were hollow. A fierce, shrill cry rose in his throat. Rarely had a vision held him so long or seemed so real. It was her. It was all tied to her—

"Move on, friend," Wally Begay said. "The *hatathli* is waiting. They will be bringing the child soon."

Cody blinked, and the world shifted slightly. His skin tightened; breath filled his lungs. With regret he turned his gaze away and met those of the young Navajo behind him. "My apology. Yes, we should hurry." He disappeared into the hogan.

Carol discovered she was sitting on a rock, hands wrapped around her knees. She felt as if she'd run a marathon, climbed the mesa behind her, carried all the sand it took to fill the desert. She couldn't move. In exhaustion, she laid her cheek on her knees and closed her eyes.

Now the chants, which had sounded so monotonous to her just moments before, unraveled into complicated rhythms that evoked images of clouds and deer, wind and rain, and then . . . a child, playing, singing, laughing. Carol trembled, eyes closed tightly as she focused on the sweet, foreign sounds of the voices, flutes, and drums. Just when she'd think she'd found the rhythm and could follow it like a safe path through the desert, it would shift and change and become a waterfall, a bird, the wind, or the child again. It left her lonely; it filled her with pain and longing. And it opened a door in her heart.

Feelings rose from deep within her soul, from the secret places where she'd hidden her emotions: The grief and loss and sorrow of that earlier time, fear, loneliness. She knew what it was like to lose a child. Her soul reached out to these people. Her heart opened to them. Oh, if only she didn't feel so alone. If only she could slip outside her skin and join the singers in the warmth and light of the hogan. If only she could soar as high as heaven and deliver her prayers herself. . . .

"It is the stones in your heart," a voice said. "That is all that keeps you from flying."

Without moving, afraid she was about to be reprimanded for intruding, she opened one eye. A pair of moccasins appeared, toe-to-toe with her own dusty boots. Nervously Carol looked up.

The old man smiled. "You are welcome as a guest. Many come from far and wide to share the blessings of a sing. Tonight, when it is over and the child is well, ask for a feather from a prayer plume. It is an eagle feather, the 'breath of life.' It should be yours because you will soar with the eagle."

Without thinking, Carol lifted her face, her throat tight with tears. "I can't."

"Yes. Forgive yourself. Take the stones from your heart." He held out his hands.

Carol drew back. "What do you mean? What do you want me to do?"

"You already have all the answers. Listen to your heart. Fly with the eagle." He smiled, his old face creasing along well-marked folds. "It is time to live your life."

Carol covered her face with her hands, not wanting to hear his words, not wanting to think about what they might mean. "I'm afraid. I don't understand you. And you're scaring me—"

But her anger was wasted. When she opened her eyes, there was no one there.

She drew a shaky breath and looked at the entrance to the hogan. Again she wished she, too, could slip inside and join the others. Should she follow the old man? Was that what he meant? But caution kept her seated, hands pressed against the hard surface of the rock. Yet she had to do something . . . something to help Leonard's child. She could not simply sit here alone, waiting, hoping.

Dropping onto her knees, she folded her hands and whispered a prayer. It wasn't very formal; the words weren't elegant or studied. But it came from her heart, carried by the tenderness and love she'd longed to offer to a child for all these years, a mother's desperate prayer. "Please, please . . . let the child be all right. Bless her little soul and keep her safe—"

A sound broke her concentration. She looked across the clearing and saw a man slip from the lighted interior of the hogan into the surrounding mist. He was there for an instant, a tall, broad-shouldered silhouette, and then his form seemed to shift and change. Winged and wondrous, his heart bursting with the power it alone could draw from the universe, an eagle leapt into the sky, climbed higher and higher in a great widening circle, and disappeared over the mesa.

Carol squinted into the dimness, her breath caught in her throat. A coincidence, that was all she had witnessed: Cody stepping behind the boulders, scaring an eagle, and the great bird bursting into flight. That was all. Any second now she'd be able to breathe again, and her pulse would slow to the steady beat of the drums. Any second now . . .

There was a sudden stillness, a tremor of expectation, and then the powerful beat of unseen wings.

She jumped in fright. There was a piercing cry from the hogan, a joyous shout. The drumbeat quickened; the voices lifted higher and higher, buoyed with joy and celebration. Women's voices rose highest of all, like flutes singing in thankful chorus to the sky. And then everything hushed. Carol felt the tears slide from the corners of her eyes, and knew other women were weeping, too, round cheeks wet with tears of relief. She felt their nearness, shared their emotion. For a second, she was one of them.

"Are you all right?" Cody's voice was a hoarse whisper, ragged and disembodied.

Carol gasped and jumped again, hands flying to her chest where her heart bumped and jumped like a wild thing caught in the cage of her ribs. "Fine . . . now." She leaned forward, squinting up at him.

He stepped farther back into the mists and shadows, but she'd caught enough of a glimpse of him to know he looked as exhausted as he sounded.

"Cody?" she whispered. "Are *you* all right? What are you doing?"

"Nothing . . . I . . . I'm not sure. I'm going

back inside. Are you okay out here alone?" Behind him, the drums had begun again, quick and lively.

Carol glanced from the hogan to Cody and back again. "Will you be finished soon?" she asked, suddenly desperate to touch him, to have him touch her. Now, with whatever had happened already fading into mist and memory, she was reluctant to be out there by herself. The emotional intensity of the ceremony had left her strangely unnerved and terribly vulnerable. Her habitual self-reliance had vanished like smoke. "I . . . I think maybe I'll go wait back at Edna's car. Would you please tell her I'll be there?"

Cody took a step toward her, but the drums demanded his return. He frowned, fighting the desire that racked his weary body. "I'm sorry. I've got to go back in. I . . . I think she's going to be all right."

"I know. The old man—the one who arrived late —he said that after the ceremony was over and she was okay, he said I could ask for an eagle feather off the . . . um, prayer plume, I think he called it? Could you get me one?"

Cody stepped out of the darkness, all the muscles along his lean, beautiful body taut with tension. "What old man, Carol? What are you talking about?"

A chill climbed her spine, a cold fingernail of fear. "You know, the old man in the mocassins and beaded shirt," she answered weakly, standing up all wobbly-kneed and ornery. "I *saw* him. You must have been too busy to notice him, too involved in the sing. But he was here. He talked to me . . . very seriously, just like the last time. I . . . I mean, last time I know it was just a dream, but this evening I . . . I mean . . ." With a little sound of dismay, Carol sat back down.

Cody lifted her by her elbows, pulling her tight against his chest. He cupped her chin and tipped her face up to his. "Are you afraid?"

"Yes."

"Of what?"

"Of everything. Most of all of you," she whispered, her breath escaping in little puffs through her parted lips. "Of myself. Of what could happen—"

He bent his head, and his lips captured hers, his kiss thrilling her, stilling her. His mouth was rough, his teeth bruising the tender flesh of her inner lip, his tongue fierce and probing. Then he tore his lips away. "What *will* happen! Wait for me. Sit here and wait for me. I have to go in and finish the sing, see that she's well, help with the last rituals. But then there's someplace I want to take you. I want you to come to my ranch with me. Tonight."

"No. I can't. Besides I don't know what's happening and I don't like it. I . . . I need to get back. I need to—"

"For once, just once, please don't argue with me, Lonesome!"

She didn't have the strength to argue, was *afraid* to argue, given what she *thought* she'd seen. She nodded, eyes wide as she watched him disappear into the hogan.

The mist thickened.

Carol lost track of the time; she may even have

dozed off. Then the women came by, the mother carrying the child wrapped in a blanket, the others moving gently behind her in a lovely, soft-stepping line.
Their voices were quiet and flutelike in the approaching dusk. They all passed by without looking at her,
but just when she thought she really must be invisible,
Edna turned and signaled to her. "Come," she whispered. "Come with me."

Like a fairy-tale princess set free from a spell,
Carol blinked and caught her breath. She darted for-
ward, her feet barely touching the ground. "Yes, wait!
I'm coming."

Within an hour she was sitting safely seat-belted
into the front of Edna's Ford. The desert was locked
safely outside the windows. The sing, the village, *Cody
Briggs*, all of it was far behind her; the Ocotillo was
just minutes ahead. Good-bye to eagles and magic
and drums and old men who appeared out of nowhere. And hello to air-conditioning and Muzak.
Carol caught her elbows in her hands and held on
tight, willing her trembling body to behave.

Edna kept her eyes on the road ahead, too polite
to ask any questions. But when they pulled up in front
of the hotel, she cleared her throat and said softly, "It
was very kind of you to want to help. The child did
open her eyes once. Perhaps the fever will break tonight. I will tell you when I hear any news."

"Thank you." Carol nodded, wanting to say more
but afraid to speak. She felt utterly confused, defenseless . . . more than a little frightened. This must be
how people felt during an earthquake, she thought,

with the ground shaking under their feet and the world tumbling down. It was hard to tell reality from fantasy, and impossible to know where to step next.

She didn't like it one bit. Not her. Oh no, she liked her life all neat and predictable, safely under control. She needed that. She wanted that. . . .

"I have to go in to work," Edna said in her soft, polite way.

Carol laughed nervously, biting her lips. "Yes. Me too. Of course. Thanks again for taking me, Edna." It took two tries, but she got the car door open and slid out.

They walked in together, without speaking, each lost in her own thoughts.

TEN

That night Carol barely slept a wink. The old worries were there, her memories intensified by the rapidly approaching anniversary of her grief. But on top of that were new confusions. She could not get the ceremony, the eagle, nor the old man's words out of her mind. And Cody Briggs was at the center of every image, every thought. It was as though his magic could haunt her even when he was far away. Her whole world was being turned upside down, and she desperately wanted to set it straight right away.

At nine A.M. she fled the empty quiet of her little room, the turmoil of her thoughts, and hurried to work. She was covering the concierge desk but, as always, she kept her attention scanning the lobby, keeping tabs on the comings and goings of the guests, the operation of the front desk, the bell staff posted near the front door.

There was no missing the tall, bushy-haired, middle-aged man who arrived carrying his own suit bag, a heavy topcoat slung over the other arm. He darted inside as if a heat devil was on his heels, red-faced and perspiring. He took a step up to the front desk then froze, turned, and sprinted toward the display cases behind Carol.

"He *is* here! I *can't* believe it. Cody Briggs working for a hotel! Impossible!" He was talking to himself, shaking his head, his shoulders thrust forward as he examined every shelf of artifacts. "My God, what a collection. Only Briggs . . . what an eye! What talent! What incredible luck to find him!"

"Can I help you?" Carol had approached him carefully from behind, wondering if this ordinary-looking man might be some kind of lunatic, or merely another former guest determined to have a repeat of a Briggs tour.

"What? Pardon me?" The man spun. He pointed a finger at the nearest case. "Where is he? Where's Doctor Briggs?"

Carol smiled politely. "I'm sorry, but he's not working today. Perhaps I could take a message—?"

"No, a message won't do. I must see him." But faced with Carol's polite coolness, he relented. "Okay. Yes, please. Get a message to him as soon as possible. This is very important." He had dropped his suit bag on the floor, tossed his overcoat on top of that, and was hurriedly slipping a business card out of a small leather folder. Reaching into his breast pocket, he took out a Montblanc fountain pen, uncapped it, and jotted a note on the reverse side of the card. He

held it out, then hesitated. "Are you personally ac-
quainted with Doctor Briggs?"

Carol arched one perfect blond eyebrow. "Yes.
He's an employee here."

The man groaned. "Unbelievable. Okay, and
you'll be seeing him today?"

Carol folded her arms, her face set. "I honestly
don't know whether or not Mister . . . I mean, Doctor Briggs will be in today or tomorrow. I'm afraid
today's tours have been canceled, and he is already
booked for tomorrow. You're welcome to leave the
message with me, or you could try to contact him
through the tour company or at his ranch—"

"He hasn't answered *that* phone for months." The
man growled. "No, I guess you're my best chance.
And your name?"

"Carol Lawson, assistant manager in charge of
guest relations, and that includes personnel here at
the Ocotillo."

"Ah. Good title. I'm Richard Currigan. I'm also in
personnel. At Harvard. So, if you could give this to
Doctor Briggs, I'd be grateful."

Carol took the proffered card and checked the
imprint. "Harvard University?" She glanced back up
and met Currigan's pleasant gaze.

"That's us. As the old saying goes, we want Briggs
to 'pahk his cah in Hahvahd yahd.' Certainly don't
want him getting snatched up by Princeton or Yale,
now do we? So speed is of the utmost importance.
You *do* understand?"

Carol nodded coolly and set the card centerfront

on her desk. "Of course. I'll give this to him as soon as he comes in. Will you be staying with us?"

"Yes. Just overnight. I'll call down and let you know what room I'm in."

"That's all right, I can check with the desk. I hope you have a very pleasant stay at the Ocotillo—"

"As long as I don't have to set foot outside the air-conditioning I'll be fine. It was thirty-five and raining when I left Boston this morning. Who knew the desert was going to be such a hellish place?"

There goes Harvard . . . Carol thought, but bit her tongue. She merely nodded and aimed Currigan at the receptionist who looked up and smiled appropriately at his approach. "Hello. Welcome to the Ocotillo. . . ."

The rest of the morning was uneventful.

Then, on the stroke of noon, Edna Yazzie hurried in. She blew across the lobby like a small whirlwind and came to a stop in front of Carol's desk. She was breathless but smiling, and Carol found her excitement contagious.

"What is it, Edna? Good news?" She crossed her fingers and held her breath.

"Very good!" The woman's eyes were bright and shining. "Annie's fever did break during the night. When she had opened her little eyes during the sing, we all thought perhaps it was a good sign. Then the fever passed, and this morning she is awake and talking and even able to take a little food. Her face has lost that going-away look. She smiled."

"Oh," Carol whispered, feeling her eyes and nose

sting with tears. "I am so glad. I cannot tell you how happy I am. For her, for Leonard and Ray, for all of you. I'm really glad." She stopped, pressing her lips together against the tears that threatened to surface.

Edna smiled and nodded. "I know. I know that your heart was with us. Thank you."

Carol shrugged. "Oh, I didn't do anything."

"You did. You cared. That is something very important." She straightened, thinking of something, then leaned back down so that only Carol would hear. Her eyes had grown huge and round, and her whole face was suffused with color. "The child told a very amazing story when she first awoke. She said she felt as if she was floating away, up toward the heavens. She said she was scared that no one could catch her. She said . . . she *said* an eagle came flying out of the darkness, and it flew up into the sky and caught her and brought her back down safely. That is what she said." Edna cocked her head, narrowed her eyes. "That is a strange story . . . a strange dream. *An eagle*. That is a very powerful symbol to see in a dream. Very strong. Very good. Not many people ever see an eagle."

Carol let her breath out after Edna had gone. She rose from her chair, weak-kneed and dizzy. Maybe she'd better eat something, she thought, before she got back to work. Maybe that would help.

At five o'clock, the workday nearly over, Carol sat in the back office opening her mail. She was procrastinating. She didn't want to go back to her room. So she slowly opened each envelope, read every word, placed them neatly in piles arranged by importance. Then one caught her attention and made her sit up and bite her lip in thought.

In minutes she was knocking at the door to Mr. LeGrand's private office.

"Excuse me. I'll only take a moment—"

"No please, come in. Sit down. I've been wanting to talk to you, Ms. Lawson. I liked several of the suggestions you made at last week's staff meeting. Would you mind writing up a proposal for that merit-pay idea?"

"I'd be happy to. I'll get on it right away. And I was thinking of attending this weekend's mini-conference at our hotel in Las Vegas. Blair Whitney, from the home office, is going to be speaking. Last year I was in a brainstorming session she facilitated, and she's wonderful. Perhaps she can answer those questions we had on the new evaluation forms. And I think I've covered all the bases: I was able to get a reasonable round-trip fare, the house is fully staffed, and the schedules are posted. I'd be gone Friday, Saturday, and back on Sunday. I could come in for a few hours then, because Monday is my day off, and I'm afraid that this one week I can't change that. But I'd be back on schedule Tuesday morning. That is," she hesitated, fingers crossed at her sides, "if you think it's a good idea—"

"I think it's an excellent idea. I like that kind of self-motivation in an assistant manager. I'll definitely look forward to reading your report. Besides, you've been putting in extremely long hours. You know the old saying, 'all work and no play . . .' "

"Yes, of course." Carol smiled, nodding her way to the door. "Well, thank you. Then I'll see you Tuesday." She held her smile until she'd shut the door, then leaned back against the wall with a sigh of relief.

The trip was just what she needed: A quick change of scene, some career stimulation—and a good deal of distance between her and Cody Briggs. It would give her a chance to think, to catch her breath, to get her life back under control, to steady herself for the sadness of next Monday.

But . . . if it was just what she needed, then why didn't she feel better? Why did the decision make her ache all over, instead of tingle with joy? Suddenly hot tears sprang to her eyes.

Oh Lord, maybe she was having a nervous breakdown. No, she wouldn't. She absolutely would not fall apart now. She hurried into the smaller office, sank into the big swivel chair, spun it around, and hunted for a box of tissues in the polished wood armoire behind her. She heard the faint sound of the heavy door opening and closing, and quickly blew her nose. "Yes? Who is it?"

"Me."

Carol spun around, lips parted in surprise. "Cody!"

He was standing with his legs apart, hands behind his back, leaning his broad shoulders against the closed door. Across the room she could feel the heat and power of his physical presence. Her heart erupted into a foolish flurry of excitement that she tried frantically to still. "What are you doing here?"

"I don't know," he answered, his voice low and husky. "I asked you to wait for me last night. You said you would."

"I didn't. I didn't say anything. I was tired and upset and—"

"And frightened?"

"Yes. I told you. I don't like it when my life feels so unpredictable, so confusing."

"That can also be called wonder . . . awe . . . astonishment."

"It can be. And that may suit some people, but not me. I don't like being taken by surprise."

"Exactly what's taken you by surprise, Ms. Lawson?"

Carol paled. Cody saw vulnerability, wariness, and caution in her lovely face. She pressed her lips together, and he saw the stubborn jut of her chin. What he didn't see, couldn't see, was the little shudder of desire that ran through her womb, or the way her heart stuttered in its beating.

Meeting those ebony eyes, Carol felt his power and struggled against it. *What had taken her by surprise?* Could she even answer that question? She licked her dry lips. "Nothing. Everything." She shook her head, turning her face so that he could see only the curve of her cheek, the pale silken spill of her hair. Her voice was so low, he had to step forward to hear it. "You frighten me."

"I don't mean to."

She shrugged off his words. "It doesn't matter. It's my problem, not yours. I need to get myself settled again, calm . . . under control."

"Why?" His voice was too close. She could feel the heat of his body, could smell the scent of him, could almost taste his mouth.

"Because—" She gasped in exasperation, swinging around in the chair to face him head-on. "Because I say so. Because that's the way I want my life. Just because."

He grinned at her, that brash curve of his lower lip that pulled down one corner of his beautiful mouth, that glint of white teeth. It made her knees weak, even though she was sitting down.

Feigning a calm she didn't feel, she turned back to the desk and began gathering up her mail. "Cody," she said without looking at him. "You need to excuse me. I have to finish up here, and then I have to recheck the schedules for the next few days. I'm going away for the weekend and—"

"Where?" he demanded, the grin wiped from his face. "Where are you going?"

Carol frowned, annoyed by his tone, by the sheer arrogance of the man. Why should she have to explain anything to him? But she merely lifted her chin. "I'm going to Vegas. To the PalmResorts property there."

"Why?"

For an instant, a heartbeat, she thought of tossing out some smart answer, playing with him a bit—he looked so totally surprised, so incredibly off balance. Let him get a taste of his own medicine, since he was so sure he liked surprises. A little shiver of excitement made her breasts peak and tingle. But one look into his blazing black eyes chased the thought away.

Pushing away from the desk, she tucked her hair behind her ear. "A business trip. I'm going to a conference offered by the home office."

"Don't go."

She closed her eyes, steadied herself, then looked up at him through her lashes. "I want to go. I *asked* to go. This is all happening too quickly for me. It's all too strange and overwhelming. I need time alone—"

"Don't go, Lonesome," he said, closing the few inches of space left between them. His hands were on the arms of the big swivel chair. He wasn't touching her, but his breath was warm on her face, his body too close to ignore. "Don't go. Don't run away. It won't solve anything, *shicho*."

Suddenly her stomach was jumping with butterflies; her palms were wet. "Cody, I'm going. I am leaving tomorrow and that is that. You have absolutely nothing to say about it."

"Maybe I won't say a word. Maybe I'll just *do* something." He lifted her out of her chair and crushed her to his chest, his mouth opening over hers with a passion that tore her breath away. She couldn't resist him. Her lips parted and their tongues met, tasting each other with a hunger that stunned Carol with its fierceness. She moaned softly against his lips even as she struggled to free herself from his embrace.

Finally, breathless and trembling, she tore herself away.

Glaring up at him, she fought to still the racing of her heart. She searched his dark eyes, anger rising and ready to explode at the first glimpse of his arrogance, but instead they burned with a tenderness that completely unnerved her.

She reached a hand out behind her and leaned back against the desk, angry, her lips trembling. "And what was that supposed to prove?"

Cody frowned. "I don't need to prove anything. I just want to wake you out of this sleep you're in, this waking nightmare. You pretend everything's all right, but it isn't, Lonesome. And you deserve better. You've got to fight for something better, even if it's painful. Even if it frightens you. *Even* if it doesn't seem to make sense in your sane and rational world!"

Carol shivered and closed her eyes. What was real? What was sane? At the moment she didn't seem to have a clue.

"Here," he said. "I brought you something."

Before she could react, she felt the whisper of a touch along her cheek, and behind her eyes there was a brightness, suddenly eclipsed by a fierce, dark shadow . . . the beat of wings.

Carol caught her breath. Looking down, she realized that Cody was holding her hand in his, her palm turned up, and lying against her skin was a single bronze feather.

"'The breath of life' the Navajo call it. It's an eagle feather—"

"I know," Carol said softly.

Cody looked at her strangely.

With a heartfelt sigh, Carol shrugged and shook her head.

Cody said the words aloud. "The old man told you?"

Running a fingertip along the feather, Carol bit her lip. "An old man who wasn't there, telling me things I don't understand. It's impossible."

"Depends on how you—"

"—define the possible. I know." Carol sighed in exasperation. "I like to define it by what I can touch, taste, see, and smell."

"That makes the world very small and dull."

"*I* like it that way."

Cody laughed, a soft, husky sound that washed over her like rain. "No, you don't. I can tell. I can taste it in your kiss. I could see it in you last night at the sing. You were openhearted and trusting, brave, curious. You're a dreamer and a seeker."

"No, I'm not."

Again he laughed. "Okay, then explain the old man."

"It's easy," she snapped, crossing her arms over her chest. "I dozed off. I was tired. Nervous. I must have fallen asleep."

"Most people don't see elderly Native Americans wearing ceremonial dress in their sleep. They don't dream of eagle feathers and know they're called 'the breath of life.' Did he say anything else?"

Carol stubbornly turned around and started to fiddle with the mail on her desk, but Cody caught her shoulders in his big hands and turned her back to face him. "He did, didn't he? What else did he say?"

"Nothing. Just nonsense. Look, I've got work to do."

"So none of this means anything to you? That's what you're going to say? That's what you're going to pretend?"

Carol pulled away and circled around the desk, putting its broad wood top between them. While all of this bothered her more than she wanted to admit, she was determined not to let him know. Already he'd gotten too close; his power had invaded her heart, her soul. But that didn't mean she couldn't fight back.

"This conversation is finished, Cody. Thank you for bringing me the feather; it's beautiful. I'll keep it as a memento. But that's that."

"Native Americans seek visions," Cody said softly as though her words meant less than the breath it took to say them. "They believe a vision has great power, and great meaning. I've often sought a vision myself these last years, in the sweat lodge, on the mountaintop. I had one last night. And I think you did also. I think what you saw is a powerful vision, whether you call him a force of nature, or destiny itself. He's leading you somewhere."

"Where?" Carol asked in a tiny voice.

Cody smiled. "Toward happiness, *shicho*. To your future."

Carol shivered, goose bumps rising along her arms. Stubbornly, with a brusk and careless gesture, she rubbed them away, then tossed back her hair. "Well, they're going to have to find me in Vegas." Gathering up her mail, she turned to face Cody, her blue eyes looking square into his dark ones. "I've got to go."

"Don't go."

"Good-bye, Briggs." As she walked to the door, a small card fluttered from the pile she was holding and fell to the floor. Carol knelt and retrieved it, then held it out to Cody. It was Currigan's business card. "I almost forgot. This is for you."

Cody gave it a cursory glance. "Oh. Dick. I'll get back to him."

"He's in room six-nineteen. He's waiting to hear from you."

"Yeah. Thanks."

Carol studied his face, looking for a reaction, but his expression remained unreadable. Darn him, the man could be stone when he wanted to. "Harvard," she said finally. "That's pretty impressive."

"It has a wonderful anthropology department."

"So." She shrugged, wishing she could stop talking but unable to control herself. "Are you going to accept the position there?"

He turned and stared out the window. She watched his back, the set of his broad shoulders, the way his long, loose hair brushed against his shirt collar like so many dark, rough feathers. As he began to turn back to face her, she could see the muscles jump along his jaw. "I had been. There, or somewhere else in the northeast." His dark gaze swung back to linger on her face. "But now I don't know. It would mean leaving the desert. It would mean losing things I love."

His use of the word, and the power of his glance, stole her breath away. Why . . . *how* could he keep doing this to her? Why did she let a word, a look creep into her heart and disturb her so? This was her life, these were her feelings, and she could control them. She had to. She'd done it very successfully for nine years, and she wasn't going to be defeated now.

Backing quickly to the door, she reached behind her and found the doorknob. "I'm sure you'll make the right decision, Cody, and of course I wish you luck."

"Wish me happiness," he said softly. Or did he? He didn't seem to move or change expression. But she could feel his strange and unexplainable power reaching out to invade her mind, her heart, her very soul. If this was magic, she didn't want any of it.

She left then, hurrying through the lobby, racing to her room, her thoughts whirling, her body aching with longing. He didn't follow. She knew he wouldn't. Yet she couldn't help but glance behind her once, twice, and again. Around her the desert was growing dark; mesas burned on the horizon, catching the last rays of the sun.

She shut her door on all of it, and yanked her suitcase out of the closet. In Vegas she'd be able to think, to relax, to set everything straight in her mind. And then she'd be strong enough to get through next

Monday, the twenty-fifth. Concentrating on only that thought, she slid two dresses onto the travel hangers, folded a slip, bra, and panties into her lingerie bag, gathered her toiletries. But deep inside, like a drum, her blood pounded fiercely through her veins.

ELEVEN

Edna waved from the front desk as Mr. LeGrand walked Carol to the taxi.

"Say hello to Martin Bennett for me if he's there. And Oliver. And Janelle Diaz."

"I will."

"And enjoy yourself. That group is known to party when the meetings are over."

Carol bit back a smile. She could see Roger LeGrand "partying." The thought hurried her steps. The cab was waiting, its motor running.

Carol slid inside. "Airport please. Continental departures." And she was off.

She felt a bone-deep exhaustion and was glad that for a few hours at least no one expected anything of her. She was only required to sit back and wait. She could do that . . . *that*, but no more. She felt as if she were the eye of a hurricane, with winds of emotion whirling around her.

Pushing her fingers through her hair, she left little neat ridges in the pale spun gold. Her hands trembled. Luckily no one was there to see. Soon . . . soon it would ease. "It's only the time of year," she said to herself, struggling for calm. "Take a deep breath. Don't panic." And, honestly, every year was like this, a roller coaster ride of emotion heading toward this final drop into depression. October twenty-fifth. It was impossible to believe that almost nine years had passed. Nine years before, she'd had a baby . . . but instead of the love and happiness that should accompany that wonder, instead there'd been only loss and grief.

A sob gathered deep in Carol's chest. She had to press her hands to her mouth to stifle the sound. Though her shoulders shook, she didn't make any noise. She was perfectly quiet. Therefore it startled her when the cab driver gave his rearview mirror a hesitant glance and cleared his throat. "You okay, miss?"

Carol stiffened and quickly arranged her face into a smile. "I'm fine. A twinge of car sickness, but I'm fine now. Nice morning, isn't it?"

"Sure 'nuf. But the air feels funny. Sky's clear and nothin's been on the radio, but I can almost smell a storm rising. Can you?"

Carol gave a tentative sniff. "I'm afraid not. It must take a real Arizonan, and I'm afraid I'm still mostly a Georgian."

"Hey, I thought I recognized your accent. You know, I have a cousin—"

The conversation went on from there, the cabbie's words racing on as fast as the car itself. When they slid to a stop in front of the terminal, Carol gave him a generous tip. He deserved it. She hadn't had a second to worry or panic for the last half hour. Maybe she should adopt him, or at least take him with her on the plane.

Smiling slightly at the thought, she wove her way through the crowd of travelers, found her seat at the back of the plane . . . a center seat between a young woman holding a baby, and a teenager plugged into a Discman. *Why?* she thought. *Why me?*

Flight 131 to Vegas landed twenty minutes late due to unexpectedly heavy air traffic. Carol carried her bag off, grabbed a cab, and rode along the Strip amidst a storm of confusion. She was late. She was tired. This city looked like Disney World gone berserk. The streets were mobbed, and horns were blaring. And when she opened the window, it had to be one hundred and twenty degrees outside. She felt as if the storm the cabbie had predicted was racing at her heels, about to envelop her.

She checked into the hotel, tossed her suitcase on the bed, and splashed water on her face. Looking into the mirror, Carol was surprised to see that she looked perfectly normal: Cool, self-contained, calm. For a second she didn't know if the thought pleased or frightened her. Had she merely gotten so good at deception and pretense that she wore it now like a thin, plastic skin? Was it protection . . . or a trap? What was real?

The meetings and workshops went wonderfully well. Carol took detailed notes, collected handouts, shook hands with acquaintances old and new. Blair Whitney included her in a panel discussion on staff evaluations. Martin Bennett invited her to lunch. She was having drinks with Janelle Diaz at seven. It was all business as usual, adorned with smiles and pleasantries, and it hurried along on its printed, prearranged schedule.

Then why did she feel so empty? No, that didn't describe this unnerving sensation. Carol felt as though her body was there, moving around gracefully, acting quite naturally, but *it* was empty and *she* was standing outside it, invisible, watching. The feeling was eerier even than when she was at the sing, surrounded by mist. What would all these people say if they knew she'd even been there, let alone spoken to a vision, kissed an eagle-man?

She shook her head, trying to chase the thoughts away. She pinched herself through the sleeve of her silk jacket to make herself feel something. Anything. But it didn't help. She felt disconnected from herself . . . suspended . . . waiting. And at the edge of her vision, there in the corner of the room, the storm was gathering. Quickly Carol looked away and smiled charmingly at the man sitting across from her at the conference table. "I'm sorry. You were saying?"

———◈———————————◈———

Janelle Diaz, Carol, and Peggy Brown went to the lounge on the mezzanine level for drinks. The place was called "The Last Roundup," and there were lassos and lariats and rawhide whips on the walls. The bar originally came from a bordello in Albuquerque. And the drinks were served in glasses shaped like cowboy boots.

The women, laughing, slipped into a corner booth. Carol ordered a marguerita; the others had scotch. It was noisy and crowded and smoke-filled. Not a sense was left unmolested.

Carol had just taken a sip of her marguerita and was setting the glass back on the table when she saw him. He turned slowly, revealing his profile . . . dark blazing eyes. . . . She spilled her drink all over the table.

By the time she got it mopped up, he was gone.

Or had he really been there at all?

"Are you okay?" Janelle asked, trying to make herself heard above the noise.

"Yes. Of course." Carol nodded, staring nervously into the smoke.

"Hell, you look like you've seen a ghost. Or *are* a ghost! You're deadly white, but there's sweat all over your face. Gee, Carol, do you want me to call a doctor?"

Carol pressed a napkin to her forehead. She felt feverish, disoriented. What? Why? The words flashed through her brain like lightning, but every sensible thought was drowned out by the rumble of thunder echoing through her mind. She struggled to her feet. "No. I'm okay. I'm just going to go upstairs. I'm really sorry about the drink—"

"Don't worry about it. And you'll let us know if you want us to call a doctor, right?"

Happen to have a *hatathli* handy, or a sweat lodge, a sand painting or an eagle feather? she wondered fleetingly, hysteria rising, but she only shook her head. "Sure. But I'll be fine. I'll see you in the morning."

Back upstairs on the twenty-third floor, Carol jammed the plastic card into the slot, but the door wouldn't open. She tried again, leaning all her weight on the door handle, cursing under her breath. Then she realized it was her phone calling card she'd stuck in the lock. With a groan she fumbled in her shoulder bag, found the key, and finally got the door open. She wanted to laugh at herself, knew she should laugh, but there wasn't a whisper of laughter left in her soul. She felt as if she were standing at the thin, crumbling edge of the abyss, and anything—absolutely anything—would push her over. She needed a friend.

Well aware that it was eleven o'clock in Atlanta on a Friday night and that the sensible place for Jill to be was munching dessert with friends at The Cheesecake Factory, she dialed anyway.

Jill picked up on the first ring. "Hello?"

"Jill? Oh, I'm glad you're there."

"Carol? Hi! How are you?"

"Jill, I've got to talk to you. I'm really confused."

"You? 'Ms Calm, Cool and Collected?' Nothing confuses you, Carol."

She threw herself onto the bed, covered her eyes with one arm, but the tears slid out anyway. "It's an act, Jill. All of it . . . all these years. Oh, Jill, I'm a fraud."

"I know." Jill said it so softly, Carol barely heard her. She said it softly to keep it from hurting. "Carol? Carol, are you there?"

"Yes."

"Listen, whatever it is, it's okay. I know you have secrets you won't share with anyone, not even with me. I always hoped that if I was patient enough, a good enough friend, someday you'd trust me with whatever had happened to you. But you don't have to. Carol . . . do you hear me?"

"Yes," Carol answered, letting the tears slide down her face. She held the receiver so tightly, her fingers ached, but it was a minor price to pay for this dear voice at the other end of the line. "Jill, I do trust you. I love you. Really. It's . . . it's me I don't trust. I never meant to hurt your feelings."

"You haven't, sweetie. Honest. That's not why I mentioned it. I only wanted you to know that I was aware of all the baggage you've been carrying around. I would have helped if I could, and I will now. Tell me what's wrong."

"Jill . . . I think I'm losing my mind. I'm seeing

things that aren't there; I'm crying all the time. I feel as if my whole life has suddenly flown out of control."

"Maybe . . . heck, I'm no expert . . . but maybe what you need is a little less control in your life, or at least a little less effort expended at trying so hard to keep things under control. I don't know, Carol, but my life sure doesn't work that way."

"But it's safer. I . . . I don't want to make any mistakes."

"You'd have to live in a cave. On a mountain. On Mars. Oh, Carol, everyone makes mistakes. You learn from them and go on."

Carol shook her head, spilling tears onto her pillow. "Some are so terrible. What if you can't go on? What if it hurts too much, or you're too scared?"

"Carol, we're talking about what happened to *you*, right? Not some impersonal 'you' here, but Carol Lawson? Well, let me tell you, you may be hurting, and you may be scared, but you *have* gone on. You're a wonderful person. You're good at your job. You're a wonderful friend. You're a kind and sensitive human being. And I bet, if you let yourself, you could even be happy."

Carol sat up, wiping her face with the edge of the bedspread. Housekeeping would have a fit, but too bad. She shifted the phone to her other ear. "Thanks, Jill. I mean it. I didn't call for a pep talk, but it felt great."

"Good. That's what friends are for. Now . . . one thing, before I let you go. What exactly have you been seeing that isn't really there?"

"Oh . . . nothing." Carol laughed, feeling absolutely foolish, like the boy who cried wolf. "I must have been dreaming."

"Well, dreams are okay. But what I want you to do now is take three deep breaths, lift up your head, and shout, 'I am a terrific person!' Okay?"

"Jill, I'm in a room on the twenty-third floor in Las Vegas."

"Hell, nobody would probably even notice there . . . but if it makes you feel better, order room service with a glass of red wine, then get a good night's sleep. I'll talk to you soon."

"Yes, I'll call again. You take care. And Jill . . . thanks so much."

"Love ya. Bye."

She ordered chicken kiev for dinner, with rice pilaf and broccoli. A glass of cabernet sauvignon. Raspberry tart for dessert. And she didn't think about eagles, or drums, or feathers at all. She was fine. Just fine.

TWELVE

"Get in."

Cody was sitting in a black Range Rover at the curb of Continental arrivals. There were two parking tickets stuck under the left wiper blade, and the man was *not* smiling.

No one had ever looked at Carol the way Cody was looking at her now. Ferociously, like an imperious warrior, dark hair bound by a midnight-blue headband, the angular beauty of his face intensified by the shadow of a beard along his jaw. Yet there was passion, too, naked as an unsheathed blade and just about as dangerous. He wanted her, and he was going to have her.

"Get in, Lonesome," he ordered, leaning across and pushing the passenger door wide. He held out a hand, tanned and callused, and Carol took it and climbed onto the seat next to him.

It simply was not possible to say no. For once,

instinct, not thought, took control. Every attempt at normalcy vanished.

They drove north toward Carefree and on past the cutoff to the Ocotillo, then farther north toward Sedona. She'd heard about Sedona, with its towering red rocks, its magic. "A mystical place," people said; "a powerful place." One could sense things there, see things, *know* things that were hidden elsewhere.

Carol needed a touch of magic right now. She sat with her hands folded in her lap, looking like an obedient novice on her way to the convent, or like Joan of Arc on her way to the stake. But beneath her pale, calm facade a storm was raging. She let it rage, feeding it with the fuel of need and longing, wishes and desire, loss and sadness, and a prayer for salvation. The sky above mirrored her disturbance. The mountains on the western horizon were topped with dark clouds, looming, threatening. A storm was brewing. All around them the desert waited, knowing what was coming.

Cody knew.

He felt as though his emotional stronghold had been breached, all his defenses destroyed. The anger he'd carried in his chest this last year, his sense of betrayal and despair were all pushed aside by the sudden, undeniable passion he felt for this woman. It raged through his blood, his heart, his loins like the flood he knew would soon rage through the desert. Some things would bloom . . . others be destroyed in the wake of such a storm. He knew it. And he hated her for awakening him from his cold, dark, solitary fury . . . and loved her as he had never loved anyone or anything before in his life. *Love*. That was the emotion splintering the walls he'd built around his soul, leaving him as vulnerable and unprotected as any foolish boy.

He sat there, hands white-knuckled on the Rover's steering wheel, his body wet with the cold sweat of fear and throbbing with intense desire. He cursed the fact that he could no longer control his body. He was already hard, hot, burning with his unbridled passion for this woman. He fantasized constantly, thinking only of holding her in his arms, tasting her mouth, her breasts, her flesh, and burying himself deep in her sweet, moist depths. Like the storm gathering over the distant peaks, this, too, was inevitable.

He would have her. He would make love to her, and make her admit her love for him. He *would*, or all that was fierce and fine and real within his heart would shrivel and die in this drought of loneliness. She was his destiny, the one with whom he'd travel the *biké hojoni*, the trail of beauty. A man could not do that alone, not with pain in his heart and bitterness eating away at his soul. Nor could a woman alone, hurt and frightened. But together . . . together they formed the two halves of the whole. He knew that now.

"Cody?" Carol whispered, stealing a glance at his forbidding profile. "How did you know what flight I'd be on?"

"I checked with LeGrand. He had your schedule. I got here early this morning and met every flight.

Doesn't make a lot of sense, I know, but I couldn't seem to help myself." Scowling, he tried to hide the rawness of his emotions, but they were too real to be contained. "Surprises the hell out of me too. But I haven't been thinking all that clearly lately."

Carol's hard-won calm deserted her. "Cody, please," she begged. "I told you, things are happening too quickly for me. Too powerfully. And this is a difficult time for me anyway. I need you to slow down. I'm feeling all confused—"

"I'll fix that. I'm going to make it all very simple, Carol. There's going to be you and me and nothing else."

"Don't be a fool, talking like some naive cowboy with nothing to worry about but his horse and his cattle—"

"I wish things were that damn simple." Cody swore. "I'd give my right arm to have nothing tougher to handle than a thousand ornery cows. But we are going to hash this out, you and me, and we're going to get past it and on to what's waiting."

She flung herself back against the door. "Nothing is waiting, Cody Briggs!"

He smiled grimly at the road unwinding ahead. "The future's waiting, Lonesome. Like it or not."

She wouldn't speak to him for the rest of the trip. She sat, arms crossed over her chest, knees tight together, for the next thirty miles. Her body felt feverish, jumpy; her emotions were shattered. She loathed her lack of self-control. The minute they got to this ranch of his, she'd call a cab and get the hell out of there.

But the minute they got to the ranch he flung the gears into park and leaned across her, his chest pinning her to the seat as he mashed down her door lock. "Don't give me any trouble here, Lonesome."

She snorted in derision. "Get off me, Cody. Are you crazy? Where are your manners?"

"Shot to hell, woman! You've blown my world to pieces, and manners were the first thing to go. I can't see straight, let alone remember to say please and thank-you."

"Then it's a damn lucky thing I've still got some self-control."

"What you call self-control is nothing but grief and anger. But like I said, we're going to fight on through that. I'll let you carry the past with you this little bit longer if you've got to, Lonesome, but we're gonna face it, deal with it, and banish it to hell. Inside the future's waiting, and we're going on in. So slide out my side or step out nice and walk up those steps, but don't give me any trouble. If you run, I'll catch you, sling you over my shoulder, and carry you in."

Before she could get out more than a squeak of protest, he cupped her chin in his palm, his dark eyes daring defiance. "God help me, I'm serious, Carol. I haven't had a wink of sleep since you sprang your little trip to Vegas on me, whenever the hell that was. Thursday? Yeah . . . well, it's Saturday, and I am one tense, edgy *hombre*."

He didn't bother to state the fact that he was also

aroused to the point of recklessness. He'd been hard with desire for days . . . nights . . . it seemed like forever. The memory of the other women he'd slept with had vanished. None of that mattered any longer. There was only *this* woman, her scent, her skin, her soft breasts flattened beneath the hard wall of his chest. He wanted her, needed her, ached for her.

The obviousness of his desire drew the tiniest of smiles to Carol's lips. The fierce pressure of his arousal thrust against the top of her thighs, and suddenly she was wet there, aching. She couldn't help herself; this obsession was mutual, and obsession it must be, or some kind of spell he'd cast on her. Her skin shivered with excitement. She shouldn't go into the house with him, but his breath on her lips stunned her, and she nodded like someone hypnotized by a single magic word.

And then, as she started up the wide stone steps which emerged from the hillside, she looked at Cody's house for the first time. Sitting on top of a red sandstone hill was a huge log structure with a double-peaked roof and windowed walls that looked across the valley at the towering red cliffs and pinnacles for which Sedona was famous. At noon the cliffs were drenched in gold, molten and shining, fabulous shapes that transfixed the eye and teased the imagination.

And the house itself almost defied description. It had been designed to merge with the landscape, to rise from it as another natural element growing out of the rock on which it sat, a beacon to travelers heading north to the Grand Canyon or south into the desert. The imposing double-door entry and wide stone porch lured Carol up the stairs. Between her and the horizon she was now able to see the rest of Cody's ranch, the barn, paddocks, a double corral, and the fine, sleek shapes of a dozen or more horses. "What a beautiful place," she whispered.

Cody looked around as if surprised to find it all there just as he had left it. Or surprised to find himself in the real world at all. "It is, isn't it? Rancho Encantado. Home." He pushed the door open. "Come in. Come on, *shicho* . . . I won't bite. Yet."

Carol stepped inside but stopped short, ready to bolt.

Cody blocked the exit with one lunging step. "You've got a choice, Carol," he said in a voice roughened by desire. "Sit down on the couch and talk to me or—"

"Or what?" she dared him.

"Or I don't know what, dammit! I haven't known what since I first set eyes on you. But I do know what my body's telling me. And if I follow that lead, I'll take you upstairs and make love to you for the rest of the day, for days without end."

"You wouldn't dare!"

Their gazes locked and held, blue fire and black storm, the air around them charged with unleashed emotion. Primitive fury and wild love. Despair, desire, and defiance. They were only inches apart now. She could feel the heat rising off his body, carrying the musky male scent of arousal. She flared her nostrils and sucked in his smell. It flowed through her like liquor, hot and potent. She wanted him. She had to touch him, taste him, feel him inside her. Carol moaned and squeezed her eyes shut.

Hiding her face, she tried to turn away, but Cody was faster. He caught her upper arms in his hands, his fingers pressing into her tender flesh. The feel of her warm, silken skin sent lust spearing through him. He had to have her. Had to feel her breasts in his hands, her nipples firm against his palms. The thought of sliding his hands down over her ribs, over the lucious curves of her buttocks, between the silken columns of her thighs maddened him. With a low growl, he pulled her against him. A shudder of delight shook him. Not all his fantasizing had prepared him for the way she actually felt, the smell of her hair, the warmth of her radiating through his skin. In a spasm of passion, his hands tightened on her arms, pulling her closer yet.

Carol struggled in his embrace, a desperate but hopeless battle against her own emotions. She wouldn't let him know how totally she wanted him. She wouldn't let him see how her body awoke and yearned for his, her skin electrified by his touch, her breasts swollen, her nipples aching points of fire. She wouldn't! She'd crush her heart, tear it out, and destroy it before she'd let it fall into some man's cruel grasp again.

Feeling her struggle so desperately against him drove Cody mad. Didn't she know how much he loved her? He'd never hurt her. He'd take away all the hurt she carried. Muscles rigid, he held her away at arm's length, dark eyes burning. "Carol, listen to me—"

"I won't!" she sobbed. "Nothing you can say will make any difference." With a cry she tore from his arms and staggered toward the door.

Cody caught her from behind, his arms wrapping tight around her chest as he pulled her back against him. He pushed his face into her pale hair, his lips brushing her ear. "I love you, Carol. Listen to me, hear me!"

"No, I can't, I can't," she wept, her slender fingers tearing at his hands.

"You will. Because we're one, you and I, two halves of a whole. I can't live without you, *shicho*, any more than you can live without me."

"You don't know—"

"But I will. Soon. But first you have to know how much I love you, and that you can trust me completely."

"No. . . ." she wailed, but already Cody had turned her gently within the circle of his arms, and his mouth found hers, his breath filling her lungs, his tongue tantalizing hers. And her fear loosened its hold on her. It was as if she'd been wearing some tight, choking garment for nine years, some terrible second skin that bound and hurt her, and suddenly it slid away. She didn't understand, couldn't trust what was happening, but her senses woke and quelled her fear.

The realization swept through her, shattering her. It left her exposed, terribly alive to every touch, every

movement, every sensation. His lips were warm and
moist now, wet with the taste of her own mouth, the
two mingled together as her tongue swept over the
probing sweetness of his, as her lips pressed hungrily
against his. She could drink his breath down into her
lungs and feel it fill her, sustain her. His beard was
rough; it scratched against her cheek and chin. And
what was that sound, that low growl of desire? Did it
come from his throat or hers?

"Cody . . ." she breathed his name against his
lips and felt his arms tighten in a spasm of longing.
Head swimming, she felt the same magic force.
"Cody . . ."

He took her hips between his hands and pulled
her closer, the feel of her inflaming him with exquisite
agony. The span of her hips fit snugly between his
powerful thighs, and his arousal was a hot insistence
against the soft, feminine curve of her belly. When
she wriggled against him, fire shot along every nerve
ending in his body, and he groaned in pain. But when
she stiffened nervously in his arms, trying not to move
at all, the pain became unbearable.

"That's it," he muttered, and without warning he
swung an arm under her knees and lifted her up.

Carol gasped in surprise, but found her breath
sipped from her lips by his fierce, demanding kiss.
Then he caught the tip of her tongue between his
teeth, worrying it playfully, the pleasure so startling
and erotic, she found herself licking her tongue over
his sweet, smooth lips, thrusting it inside, nibbling at
the corner of his mouth.

Cody gave a husky shout of laughter and kissed her again, taking the steps to the second landing two at a time. To Carol, the ground seemed to simply drop away, and she was flying, soaring . . . until with an unceremonious plop he tossed her onto the middle of his huge bed and dropped down next to her. Her pulse was racing, her head spinning. The ceiling was covered in stars . . . or were those fireworks exploding behind her closed eyes?

"Open your eyes, Lonesome. Look at me," Cody whispered, his breath raising goose bumps from neck to knee.

She couldn't resist him. She could only do what he asked. She found herself looking into the warm, revealing depths of his Indian-dark eyes. "I love you," he said. "I think I've loved you all my life and was just waiting to find you."

Carol pressed her hands to her eyes, trembling.

"No, don't hide from me, Lonesome. No more hiding, ever. Here . . . we'll start with me. Look . . . I'm not afraid anymore. The walls are all down. Whatever I feel, you'll feel. Here . . ." He took her hand in his, pressed his lips to her palm, then blew a warm breath against her skin. "That's my spirit, the man inside. And the rest of me, all you see and feel, all you will see and feel, I give to you also as a gift."

His words stole her breath away, banishing fear. Without thinking, she drew her hand down the side of his face, her fingertips memorizing every line and angle.

Cody curved over her, his mouth tracing the out-

line of her lips, her brows, the fine slope of her throat
from chin to collarbone. He trailed hot kisses over her
skin, licked her with his raspy tongue, then blew his
breath across each sensitized nerve ending until Carol
shivered and squirmed against the soft, thick quilt.
His hands found the top button of her blouse and
opened it. The others followed. His callused fingertips lingered erotically over the rise of her breasts,
then slid just the littlest bit under the lacy top of her
bra. Against the delicate lace, her nipples peaked,
tight and aching. Her breasts felt full and tender; one
touch would make her cry. Yet if he didn't touch her,
if she didn't soon feel his hands cupping her aching
flesh, she would die. Arching her back, eyes squeezed
shut, she moaned softly deep in her throat.

His mouth covered hers, his tongue thrusting into
her waiting mouth. Again he caught the tip of her
tongue between his teeth, but this time he sucked on
it, hard, his desire fierce and unremitting.

Then, taking his mouth away, he grinned at her,
his dark hair falling around his shoulders, his teeth
flashing.

Eyes bright as flames, Carol reached up and pulled
his headband off, letting his hair fall across her face,
her throat. The rough, blunt edges were like a thousand fingers touching her, stirring her, waking something deep within her.

Cody saw it. He knew.

Eyes dark as coals, small flames glowing at their
centers, he drew his gaze slowly down from her face
to her breasts, and parted the edges of her blouse, the

silk sliding like water over her skin, over the curve of her ribs, baring her abdomen. He began there, his fingertips grazing over her, lighting tiny fires until her whole body was aflame with desire, his fingers moving slowly up each rib until they brushed against the soft underside of each breast and that same small sound of helpless abandon gathered in her throat.

Carol ploughed her fingers through his hair, feeling the heat of his scalp, the perfect curve of bone beneath. She stroked his neck, feeling the sweat of his arousal lying on his skin. Her hands closed on the ropes of muscle crossing his shoulders; curved over her as he was, his weight resting on elbow and hip, his shoulders were tense and knotted. His strength excited her. She pushed back the collar of his shirt and kneaded her fingers into his hard flesh, then leaned up and bit him lightly on one shoulder, her teeth leaving the faintest of marks on his bronzed skin. Oh God, she wanted to mark him more wantonly than that, wanted suddenly to draw her fingernails down his back and raise red welts, wanted to knot her fingers in his hair and draw his head back until she could find his mouth and bite hard on that sensual lower lip and make him growl again deep in his chest . . . her cougar, her wild animal, trapped and tamed by her touch.

His touch set her on fire. Cupping her breasts through the flimsy lace, he circled his thumb over her nipples, one and then the other, slowly, maddeningly, each circle making the nipple tighten and harden more, each touch stroking like fire across her aching breasts. Then suddenly his fingers stopped, touched for a moment on the tiny clasp there between her breasts, and the lace parted.

Cody held her gaze a moment, his own burning with a fierce, wild promise. Then his gaze traveled down to her breasts. The bra had fallen partly open, but lace still covered her nipples. A moment. And then he bent his head and kissed her, one nipple and then the other, through the lace. She felt his warm breath flow over her sensitive flesh, making it pucker, feeling the tightening all through her, right to her womb. She'd never felt such pleasure before, such unbearable pain. He pushed the lace aside, slid the thin straps down off her shoulders, baring her further. She felt his mouth on her breasts, his tongue circling her nipples, flicking back and forth like a quick, hot flame across their peaked, aching points. Then he was sucking on her, pulling at one nipple and then the other, his mouth hot and urgent, tugging fiercely, drawing waves of sensation up from her core, ripples of exquisite need and desire that swept over her and consumed her. Suddenly he dragged his mouth away.

Carol moaned in protest and desire. Her hands were clenched around pieces of the quilt, pulling at it as if it would somehow rise and cover her, hide her, but at the same time her back was arched in eager response to Cody's wandering hands. His kindling touch roamed across her skin, tracing her ribs, teasing across her abdomen, lingering for a moment at the waistband of her skirt.

Carol's heart stuttered in its beat. Her breath

stopped in her throat. *He would stop now; he had to.
. . .* She gulped air in a ragged sob as her skirt fell
undone, and she felt his fingers slide down inside,
over her waist, her belly button, beneath the silk of
her panties and down like fire over her skin. They
stopped just as they reached the triangle of soft, curly
hair there at the top of her thighs. She gasped and lay
trembling, stunned by sensations she'd never even
imagined. When his fingers stirred, caressing, explor-
ing, she caught her lower lip between her teeth and
moaned; tears slid from the corners of her closed eyes.
One more touch, and she'd explode.

Cody was trembling, all teasing gone now, his
own heart hammering like a drum in his chest. The
feel of this woman, her softness, her beauty had
aroused something unexpected within him, something
beyond pure physical desire. Her responsiveness, so
hesitant at first and yet so ardent, shook him to his
soul. He felt as though he could touch her very heart.
It made his own eyes sting with tears.

Lowering his head, his hair falling like a dark cur-
tain across her breasts and ribs, he sipped at one pink
nipple and then the other. She made a soft sound of
delight that thrilled him. Beneath his hand, he could
feel the muscles of her belly tighten and ripple, and
felt in his own body the shudders of sensation that
seized her. Gently, intimately, he grazed his fingers
across the mound of fine, curly hair. She shuddered
again, her body curving deliciously to the possessive
urging of his mouth and hand.

Carol knew that touch would shatter her into a

million tiny pieces. She was made of glass, glass laid over fire, and his hand, his mouth were fire also. His hand moved, sensually cupping her, his fingers grazing the tops of her thighs. She squeezed her eyes tighter, but her body craved his touch. She couldn't help herself. Tightening her buttocks, she lifted her hips ever so slightly, and his fingers slid into her warm, slippery cleft. She quivered and moaned, her head tossing wildly back and forth against the quilt.

Cody felt her open to his touch, and it was all he could do to keep from taking her then, sheathing himself in her hot, moist silkenness. But he pulled back, panting and gleaming with sweat, his broad chest heaving. It took him a moment to find his voice. "Lonesome, look at me. Don't be afraid. Look at the man who loves you."

Clinging to his neck, she bit at her lips, unable to silence the tremulous sound of ecstasy and fear that rose in her throat.

Before she knew what was going to happen, she felt him slide down the front of her body. His warm breath washed across her skin, making her shiver uncontrollably, and then there was the rasp of his beard against her inner thigh.

Carol swallowed a strangled cry; even her breath was held captive by the intensity of the sensations he aroused. She lay awash in a riot of emotion. Then Cody rubbed his rough cheek on her other thigh and blew his warm breath against her most sensitive flesh.

Her body opened like a rose, swelling, blooming. When he caressed her boldly with his tongue, she cried out and tried to wiggle free, but he held her hips gently, working his magic on her until she felt her body shatter into glittering shards of pure sensation.

She lay trembling, surprised to find her fingers tangled in Cody's wild, dark hair. Lifting his head, he laid his cheek on her belly. "You're like all the flowers of the desert, all petals within petals . . . so beautiful," he whispered, then gave a husky, strangled laugh. "And I'm a bee drunk on your sweet honey."

He moved back up over her body like a flame that licked its way across her flesh, rekindling her excitement to a fever pitch. Stop . . . stop . . . she meant to say, but her hands slid down his back and closed around his lean, hard hips, urging him closer. When his mouth slashed hungrily across hers, she answered with the same aching hunger.

She kissed his dark, loose renegade hair, his sensuous mouth. She kissed him fiercely, biting at his lower lip. Her hands prowled eagerly over his shoulders and back, down to his jean-clad hips, curved over the hard muscles of his buttocks. She grabbed the back of his shirt in her hands, pulled it free of his jeans, and slid her hands up over the smooth, hard muscles of his back, searing his bare skin with her fingertips. The sound that rose in his throat was echoed in hers. She'd never felt anything as erotic and powerful as the way his muscles tensed and tightened beneath her palms. She had to touch more of him, see more of him. Pushing his weight away with her small hands, she unbuttoned every one of the buttons on his shirt, then spread the cotton wide.

He was magnificent, each muscle sculpted clean and fierce. She touched him because she had to. She pushed away the thin silver chain he wore and slid her hands up over the broad slabs of his pecs, then circled his dark, small nipples with her thumbs. They grew hard in an instant. He groaned and fell back on the bed, *his* eyes closed now, gritting his teeth. With delight, Carol tugged his shirt back off his shoulders and as far down over his biceps as she could. In a quick, smooth motion Cody shrugged free of it and lay back, bare to the waist.

Carol ran her hands covetously over him, from shoulder to belly, savoring every sensation: The heat rising from his skin, the power of his chest, and the dark pelt of hair, the washboard muscles ridged across his abdomen. There was hair there, too, a thin line of dark hair arrowing down into his jeans. She pushed her fingers across his skin, feeling the hair rough and furry against the tender pads of her fingertips. Her whole body shuddered with excitement. Is that how he felt when he first touched her? Her eyelids fluttered. It was beyond words, an overwhelming mystery.

Her fingers slid beneath the waistband of his jeans, following that dark arrow. Her pulse was racing. Beneath her hand, she felt Cody's body tighten convulsively. His chest rose with an indrawn breath and stayed that way. Her hand found his sex, hot, hard, throbbing with the pulse of his heart. She felt the breath shudder out of him.

Cody bared his teeth and ground his head into the quilt.

When she touched him, he thought he was going to die. A sound escaped his throat, and Carol pulled back, startled.

Cody groaned, sweat standing out on his chest. "Oh God, don't stop now."

She couldn't even if she had wanted to. She had to touch him again, feel him fill her hand. Trembling, aching, she closed her hand on him and slid it down to the root of his power, feeling his hot, smooth skin, the incredible urgency of his desire.

Cody drew his breath in sharply, stunned into stillness.

Then, as if with one thought, two sets of hands were on his clothes, groping wildly until everything was gone and now they were both naked on the bed, their breath hot and panting; the whole room seemed to grow warm with the heat rising from their bodies. He leaned back from her, dark gaze burning into her soul, savage and gentle, loving and fierce, his sex unsheathed, thrust out hard and dangerous as a weapon.

Carol took quick, little shallow breaths through parted lips, her eyes devouring him. She wanted him, wanted to feel his power inside her, *needed* to feel him filling the emptiness inside her. With a little cry of excitement, she flung her body against his, pressing herself to his hard, hot sex. She reached down and touched him, making him moan in his throat.

They touched each other with quick, thrilling caresses, lips and hands pressed everywhere in touches that delighted and maddened both.

A sob rose in Carol's throat, a strangled cry of need and longing. She couldn't ask, couldn't find the words to ask for love; it had been too long, too awful. But her body knew, her heart knew. Writhing in silent torment, she clung to Cody's flesh, dug her nails into his back. She could feel the hard rod of his arousal and she rubbed against it, while desperate, inarticulate sounds welled up in her throat.

Cody groaned, whispering love to her, his fingers digging into her hips as he tried to slow it down, wanting to make it last for her, make it perfect. His hands cupped her buttocks, then slid between her thighs, stroking, caressing, parting her. He whispered her name over and over as she arched against him, moaning feverishly, her nails raking his skin. Bending his head, he nipped at the taut, peaked tips of her breasts and felt her body spasm with excitement. Thrusting himself away from her, avoiding her hands, he breathed her name. His breath came hard, and he was glistening with sweat, but he didn't try to enter her yet. Not yet. "Carol . . ." he whispered. "Wait. I love you. Tell me if I'm too rough. Tell me—"

With a tremulous cry, Carol pulled him back down, her hips rising to meet him. With a groan, Cody sheathed himself in her sweet, velvety heat. He could feel her muscles tighten around him, felt them clutch at his sex with a voluptuous softness that made him swell and harden until there was nothing but that wild, unbearable ecstasy.

Carol had begun to climax with his first powerful thrust, shuddering convulsions that rippled through her, starting deep inside and spreading out along her body until they consumed her. For a moment she balanced on that sharp, burning point between pleasure and pain, and then she dissolved into wet, honeyed bliss. "Cody," she cried. "Yes, oh yes . . ." Clinging to him, she wrapped her legs around his hips, drawing him deeper and deeper inside until each thrust seemed to hammer at her womb. He surged within her, filling her, completing her, carrying her past thought and fear to a perfect place where she wasn't alone, where she would never be alone again.

She felt his body tighten, his breath catch in his throat and then hiss free in the final spasm of orgasm. He kissed her long and hard on the mouth, kissed her bare shoulder, then lowered himself slowly to her side and lay with his eyes closed, breathing raggedly.

Carol lay there, her pulse still beating wildly in her throat, the echo of it just beginning to fade between her legs. She felt all muzzy and warm, drunk on pleasure, wrapped in peace. Turning her head, she let her gaze skim his beautiful body, then blinked in surprise. "When . . . how . . . ?"

He grinned at her, watching her from beneath lowered lashes. "Wanted to make sure you were safe," he whispered, cocking one arm under his head. His bicep bulged, smooth and supple.

Catching her bottom lip between her teeth, Carol touched his arm, her fingers trembling at the strength, the power lying beneath his dusky skin.

"What?" he whispered, brows swooping low.

She couldn't speak. Shaking her head, she blinked back tears.

"Come here," he said, pulling her down onto his chest. Those strong arms circled her back; his hands stroked her hair.

She shivered with delight, but even as pleasure reigned, slowly, ever so slowly, Carol could feel old emotions creep into her consciousness.

Cody was grinning, snuggling her closer still, curving his big body around hers. He pulled the quilt up over them both, thinking all was now right with the world.

THIRTEEN

Carol was lost in the deep, fathomless sleep that sometimes comes after lovemaking. She lay entangled in Cody's arms, warmed by the heat of his big body, soothed by the steady beat of his heart.

Cody watched her sleep. Looking at her filled him with a keen joy and an even sharper longing. He was hard again, restless and on edge, the heat coiling fierce and ready in his loins. She did that to him, this slim, pale girl, this lucent flame. Holding her in his arms, he was burning, burning. His breath hissed into his lungs through clenched teeth. When had it begun, this wanting? There wasn't any answer, only the fierceness of his desire.

And then she stirred. Her eyelids were tugged by dreams, and her breathing quickened to a startled flutter in her throat.

Wanting to comfort her, Cody covered her small hand with his.

Carol shot up in bed as though she'd been burned, her eyes wide and tear filled, her lips quivering. "No!" she cried, still lost in the terror of her dream. "Oh no, please don't take her away—" She swallowed back tears, looking around for a second in absolute bewilderment, then covered her face with her hands and sobbed helplessly. The sound was terrible, frightening in its utter desolation.

Cody's chest felt as though it would cave in around his heart. It hurt to draw breath. "Carol," he whispered. "Lonesome, it's all right. I'm here. I'll help you."

She pushed at him blindly. "Go away. Leave me alone!"

"I won't," he said, reaching for her, catching her in his arms and taking the worst of her blows against his chest. She struggled feebly, then collapsed against his shoulder.

"Oh, not again, not again. . . ." She wept in despair, her sobs slowing to little hiccuping sounds against his warm skin.

He stroked her hair and held her tight, and from within the dreaded familiarity of her grief, Carol felt that something was new and different. But it was too new, too different to trust. Risen so abruptly from her dream, she was frighteningly disoriented. Nothing made sense. The only thing crystal clear was the pain that had woken her, that woke her all too often from sleep. "Oh, dear God, I can't bear this." She wept.

"Come here, *shicho*. I'll help you." He held her tightly. Her pain was his pain. Her tears soaked his skin. He wanted desperately to protect her, soothe her, save her from whatever had caused this terrible loss and grief. She broke his heart. "Carol . . . oh, Lonesome, tell me what's wrong. I love you. And I know you love me."

Her breath was a gasp of fear. "No, I can't. Oh, Cody, I can't. I'm too afraid—"

Cody crushed her to his chest, smothering her words against his warm skin. His breath was in her hair. "Don't be. Oh, *shicho*, loving someone with all your heart and soul is the most wonderful thing in the world."

But she was too frightened to listen. Tears slid down her cheeks, and she didn't even bother to wipe them away. Clutching the quilt around her, she half slid, half fell out of bed.

Cody leapt after her and wrapped his arms around her, quilt and all. He would die before he let her go and suffer this alone. By sheer strength he'd hold her until she calmed down enough to talk. He cradled her against him, whispering soft words into her hair.

But Carol was quickly sliding over the edge into hysteria. Her heart was being torn apart, pulled to pieces between fear and longing. Out of habit she fought to be alone, to hide inside herself, silent and self-reliant. It was the way she'd survived since that distant, haunting morning.

But this man—this strong, loving, wonderful man —he was holding her, talking to her while the storm raged in her head, making her think, making her feel. No one had ever done that before. He woke the child within her heart, the self who wanted to trust and love, to let down the walls, to open herself to all that was possible, all that was beautiful. . . .

When he gently kissed her wet cheek, she collapsed against him, the threads of her life unraveling. She didn't know what to do.

As if his heart could read her thoughts, Cody knew what *he* needed to do. He laid her on the bed, lifted one end of the quilt and slid in next to her, his strong, hard body anchoring her to reality. Whatever haunted her wasn't going to get past his ferocious guard. Never again.

"Carol," he said, running his hands up and down her slim back. "Lonesome, I'm here. I'm going to stay with you, no matter what. It doesn't matter what you say. It doesn't matter what happened before. I won't leave you."

Carol shivered uncontrollably. She clenched and unclenched her hands spasmodically, her emotions storming through her in confusion and chaos.

Nine years of repressed grief and pain surfaced in a shattering eruption.

"Don't do this to me, Cody. Don't make me trust you. Don't let me love you!"

Dark eyes fierce and burning, he leaned over her. "Too late, *shicho*. Too late for both of us. Talk to me."

Carol tried to slide away. She was trapped, and furious. Those strong arms, that big chest, she hated them, hated the longing that rose in her throat at the sight of them, the overwhelming desire to use them as sanctuary against all that was lost and sad and empty in her life. Tears gathered on her lower lids but she blinked them away.

"What is it, Lonesome? Say it," Cody whispered, bending his head and rubbing his rough beard lovingly along her cheek.

It was such a small thing, but that touch was enough to push her over the edge.

Before she could catch herself, the past overtook her. Before she knew it was going to happen, she was back in the white, sterile delivery room under the bright lights, and the hurting had stopped and someone had placed the baby in her arms. She looked down and there was this perfect, sweet face, these tiny fingers, these tiny toes, all warm and nuzzling in her arms, and she was so happy, filled with joy. Her heart was overflowing with emotion. And then, amid a hiss of voices and hands, the baby was gone. Gone forever. Her body empty, her arms empty, the room empty . . . and she was all alone.

She'd been alone in the empty room of her memory for nine years.

Carol tried to stifle her cries, but sobs tore at her throat, frightening and embarrassing her. She pressed her hand to her mouth.

Cody pulled it away, capturing both her hands in his. "No," he whispered. "Let it out. Let it go, Carol."

"I can't!"

"You can. You have to. Let it go, *shicho*. Give it to me."

"No. I'm so afraid—"

"Stop being afraid. Right now. Here. With me," he commanded. "Tell me. Take who away?"

"My baby! It was my sweet baby!" She gave a high, wild cry of grief. "They took my daughter away."

Cody leaned across her, his weight pressing her down into the soft quilt as if by doing so he could keep her from being swept away by the raging flood of her sorrow. He used his body as a shield, as he would have if they'd been caught in the terrible storm outside. Beneath him she wept silently now, clinging to his neck as if she were in danger of drowning. Finally, minutes later, she stilled.

"Tell me now, Carol," he whispered, stroking her hair.

She hid her face against his neck, trembling.

"Tell me about your baby, Carol. What happened to the baby?"

Her arms fell limply from around his neck. She covered her eyes with one hand. "I gave her away." It was a ghost's voice, haunting and terrible.

The hair rose on the back of Cody's neck. It was worse than he'd ever imagined. "Why? Tell me. Trust me."

She shuddered. When she found her voice, it was barely recognizable as her own. "I . . . I couldn't take care of her. I was too young. I didn't have a job. I didn't have anyone. . . ."

"You were all alone?"

"Yes." She let her hand fall from her face and looked up at him, her eyes stunned with pain. "I wanted to take care of her and love her, but everyone said it made more sense . . . that it was better . . . it would be better if—" Her voice was choked off by the sudden thickness of tears in her throat.

"Better for the baby?" Cody prompted, watching her carefully, his own eyes darkened with understanding.

"Yes," Carol whispered shakily. "Better for my baby. So they took her away." Her chin quivered and tears slid from the corners of her eyes.

"A family adopted her?"

Carol nodded quickly, spilling tears in all directions.

"So she was all right. But you missed her, didn't you?"

A wail of grief broke from Carol's lips. It was a noise she'd heard inside her head for nine years and never dared let out. "Oh God, oh God . . . I miss her so much. I never got to see her smile, or hear her coo or buy her little clothes . . . Oh God . . . how could such a bad thing happen? Why did it have to happen? Oh God . . . I am so sorry . . . so sorry . . . so sorry—"

"It's all right, *shicho*. You did the best thing for your baby."

She bit her lips and turned her face away, unable to stop her tears. "I know. That's what everyone told me. That's what I've told myself. But it still hurts so much."

Cody pulled her into his arms and rocked her to

and fro, gently stroking her hair. "Shhh . . . it wasn't your fault."

She twisted in his arms. Her voice was wretched and haunted. "But it was. It *was* my fault. I wasn't careful enough. I didn't plan, I didn't think. I just went on foolishly, trusting him, believing lies. And then suddenly there was nothing to do, no safe way to go, no one to help me."

"Who was it, Carol? The man who hurt you, who was he?"

The tortured look on her face made Cody wish he hadn't asked, but he knew these memories were the poison sickening her. "Tell me, *shicho*. Who was the father? Why didn't he stay with you?"

Carol laughed bitterly, the sound no more than a hollow echo of despair. "Because he was home with his wife and children where he belonged, probably waiting for the next stupid, blind little college freshman to stand in his office door and look at him as if he were God. 'Oh, yes, your essay is extremely thought provoking and, by the way, my wife is a ball-buster but *you* are the loveliest, the kindest, the most sensitive of women. How about a little cocktail before dinner?'"

"Bastard," Cody swore. "Damn him to hell!"

Cody knew that kind of thing happened on a college campus, but he hated it. To abuse the power you had as a teacher, the trust placed in you by those young people . . . the thought disgusted Cody. It was a crime as despicable as theft or betrayal . . . a cowardice of the soul.

He waited a minute to speak, knowing his anger now wouldn't help. Instead he asked softly, "You didn't blow the whistle on him, Lonesome?"

She shook her head dumbly, fighting a fresh onslaught of tears. "I was *so* embarrassed. It was horrible. I . . . I didn't know what to do. I couldn't even think. Then . . . soon . . . there were no choices. I went to my older sister's in Birmingham, had the baby and . . . and . . ." Her voice faded. She struggled to catch her breath, but her emotions were in such turmoil it took all her strength simply not to cry. She pushed at him, fumbling with the quilt. "I don't want to talk about it anymore, Cody. I can't." Wearily she tried to slide out of bed.

"Don't, Lonesome. Wait. Let me hold you. Let me comfort you."

Carol hesitated for an instant. Maybe, oh maybe this man, this strong, wonderful man was the one she could share this with, the one heart she could trust. Her body was still filled with the feel and smell of their lovemaking. His soul was in his dark, loving eyes. Maybe . . . oh, maybe. . . .

But it was too soon, too big a leap for her wounded spirit to make. She shook her head. "Please, just let me go."

His arms tightened around her. "Don't run away now, Carol. Stay. Talk to me. Do it for your own sake, not for mine."

Fear flowed like ice through her veins. Stubbornly she pushed his hands away. "I need to be by myself. Surely you can understand that."

"I love you," was all Cody answered. He exhaled harshly, dreading the battle he knew was coming. He was tired, emotionally and physically. All he wanted to do was hold this woman in his arms and slide off into sleep, then wake with her, love her, and sleep some more. It didn't seem like such an outrageous desire. Instead he had to gear up for another round. Drawing a breath he said, "Carol, you can trust me."

His gentleness undid her. She felt the hot sting of tears behind her eyelids but fought to hide them. If she gave in now, if she fell back into those strong, waiting arms, she'd need to stay there forever. She'd need his strength to protect her, his heat to warm her, his love to make her whole. In a high, strained voice she defended herself the only way she knew how. "I don't want to trust you. It's as simple as that."

"It's not simple anymore, Carol. It's too late for that. We've got to work this out—"

"I don't want to," she interrupted. "I'm happy the way I am and—"

"Bull! You're not happy. You're miserable. Hurting. Lonely. Worn-out with sadness. I know. I wasted a year torn up with those feelings, but that's over. And in some way I can't explain, it's over because of you. You healed my heart. And I want to do the same for you. I want to help you heal. I want to bring you joy. I want to love you."

"Dammit, Cody, don't you hear me? I want to be alone now—"

"Liar," he interrupted, grinning suddenly. "You can say the words, but your body doesn't lie.

Here . . ." he said, nestling a hand under her left breast. "I feel your heart racing so sweet and quick. . . . And here," his other hand slid up between her thighs, making her catch her breath in surprise and excitement. "Here, the sweetness of our joining—"

At an absolute loss for words, Carol merely slid from the bed and pulled on the first thing she could find, ignoring the fact that his shirtsleeves hung six inches beyond her fingertips and the shirttails flapped around her knees. "I'm going to take a hot shower, dress, and go home."

"Got a boat, Lawson?" He grinned. "The roads'll be flooded by now."

Carol frowned in confusion. She tipped her head, and for the first time she became aware of the steady beat of raindrops on the roof, the far-off rumble of thunder. "How long has that been going on?" she asked softly.

"Last couple of hours, at least," Cody answered, stretching his arms over his head. His biceps bulged beneath golden skin.

Carol's mouth went dry. Her pulse raced. She tried to focus on the weather. "I didn't even hear it." She sighed, shaking her head in amazement.

"That's because you're so locked up in your sadness, nothing else exists for you, *shicho*. But that's coming to an end."

Carol flinched. "Don't do that, Cody. Please. I'm asking you, as a favor. I think . . . considering what's just happened here—" She made the smallest gesture to the bed he lay stretched across like a big, lazy wildcat. "I think I can ask that much."

"You can ask me for anything, Carol. I'd give you my life if you wanted it."

"What I want is for you to *stop* all this. Stop talking to me that way. Stop looking at me that way. I know you think this is fate, or destiny, or some other such nonsense, but it's not. I can tell you, Cody, there is no such thing. There's the things you do and the mistakes you make, and there's trying to live so you don't make any more. That's what life is. I know. Damn you, haven't you heard anything I've said to you?"

"I heard it all, Lonesome. I hurt for you. I'm sorry for what happened, but it's done. The child is okay. It's you who's still suffering. Let me ask *you* something." He leaned up on one elbow, his broad chest gleaming. "When are you going to forgive yourself and put the past behind you? It's time to live your life."

It is time to live your life! That was what the old man had said the night of the sing . . . *those very words* . . . but how? It was impossible!

Breathing hard, Carol backed up and bumped her calves on an old wooden chest sticking out of the corner. She stood there, wide-eyed and trembling, fighting against this magic, this impossible enchantment.

Cody leaned forward, the quilt sliding down around his hips, his whole body reaching for her. "Come here, Lonesome. Let me hold you. Let me love you."

Carol felt her body curving toward his, hungrily, desperately. She wanted to give in and lose herself in his embrace, to yield to the sensual pleasure and the sheer joy of being held. In his arms was the only place she'd ever tasted peace. Joined together, she'd finally felt whole. But she didn't dare.

Stiffening her shoulders, she shook her head.

Cody searched her closed face. This woman, slim as a blade of grass, fierce as a flame, she could make the sweat rise along his skin, could turn his heart inside out in his chest. Yet she wouldn't trust him.

That hurt. He was hurt and angry and now his own emotions slipped from his control. With a growl he leapt from the bed and stalked into the bathroom. "There's a guest room down the hall. Use that."

FOURTEEN

Carol padded down the hallway over Mexican tile that felt soothing to her bare feet. She needed something to cool her off. Her skin was still feverish with Cody's touch, and the taste of him still burned her lips.

She tried the first door on the right and found herself in what was obviously Cody's office, a big room windowed from floor to ceiling on its southern exposure, the glass framing a vista of red rocks and a distant horizon shadowed by clouds and mountains. Pearl-gray late-afternoon light filtered in, illuminating his desk and shelf after shelf of artifacts: Pots, weapons, kachinas, breastplates, bones, shells, and silverwork. But despite the quantity of things, there was no sense of clutter or disarray; each piece held an honored place. For a second Carol wondered what it would be like to cherish the past rather than regret it, but she quickly shut the door on that thought and the room both.

Finding the guest room, Carol tossed her clothes on the bed and headed for the bathroom. The shower was hot and stinging, and she stood under it with clenched teeth, welcoming the punishment as her just desert. Why had she ever come here? Rancho Encantado. She knew from high school Spanish what the word meant: Enchanted . . . Charmed. Oh, was the whole world conspiring against her? Was destiny toying with her? Why had she gone and fallen so completely in love with Cody?

Tears mixed with water on her upturned face as she stood there, overwhelmed by questions that seemed to have no answers.

Cody stood under the porch overhang, drinking a beer and watching the rain. He turned as Carol stepped out the door, his heart leaping at the first sight of her. It was pure happiness, an unthinking response like the flicker of fire along his veins, the tightening in his groin. He loved this woman. Seeing her, there on his porch, sent his emotions spinning out of control.

And in her wide blue eyes he glimpsed the echoing flicker of response that so thrilled his soul. Glimpsed it for a second and then it was gone. He searched her face but now her lips were pressed into a thin line, her pale brows furrowed in worry. She half turned away.

Even her voice was distant. "This is like a Georgia

rain. I never thought it could rain this hard in the desert."

"It won't last long," Cody answered softly.

"Good. I have to go."

Narrowing his eyes, Cody took a long pull on his beer. He didn't want to think about how he'd feel when she left. *What if she never came back?* He didn't think he could survive the loneliness. Didn't know if he wanted to.

"Damn!" he muttered, tipping the bottle up and draining it dry. "Damn it all." He turned and stalked into the house.

Carol wanted to go after him, wrap her arms around his waist and press her cheek against his back, right there between his shoulder blades. He'd turn . . . he'd touch her . . . their lips would meet. . . .

At the thought her body spasmed with longing and her willpower flagged. She was tired of being hard and strong. She wanted to lay her body next to his, naked and free, without fear or restraint. She wanted to open herself to him, body and soul. Adore him. Trust him. Love him and be loved in return. Could this man be her soul mate, this dark-eyed cowboy? This wild and passionate creature of moonlit mesas and stark desert? Her heart said yes. It whispered to her in a tiny voice she'd long forbidden herself to hear. But she'd laid in bed with him, she'd made love with him, she had followed her heart that far, which was so very far from the loneliness she'd known. Should she go further, that little step further into trust? Did she dare? Did she even know how?

First she had to get through tomorrow.

Rigid with tension, she turned her back on the silvery patter of the rain and followed Cody into the house.

He was in the kitchen, leaning against the sink, polishing off another beer. He merely glared at her.

Carol paused to steady her voice, then asked, "Got another of those?"

"Sure." He gestured roughly toward the fridge.

She pried off the top and took a small sip. No matter what it cost her, she intended to be as honest with him as she could be. She owed him at least that much. "Cody, once I go back to the hotel, I'm going to need some time alone. I . . . I don't think we should see each other again for a little while."

The muscles along his jaw jumped, but he took another drink before answering. "'Fraid I can't do that, Lonesome."

"You have to," she said, fighting the emotion that tightened her throat.

He shook his dark head, white-edged lips pressed together in inarguable refusal. "Only things I *have* to do are pay taxes, die, and love you until I do."

Carol's shoulders pulled together as though her heart had stopped suddenly. It almost hurt too much to talk. She struggled on, her voice trembling. "You don't understand. That's okay, I never really expected you to understand. No one could. But I know that for my own sanity, I need this time all alone. I have to get myself back together and do what I need to do these next few days. I have to go it alone. I can't afford to need anyone, to be that vulnerable. Now, I . . . I admit I feel something for you—"

"Well, that's the first sensible thing you've said," Cody drawled. "And what exactly *do* you feel?"

Carol skipped over that to what she was determined to say. "Even though I regret coming here, I guess it was inevitable, given the . . . the attraction between us. But that's it for now. No more."

"That's like telling the rain to fall backward up into the sky, *shicho*. It ain't gonna happen."

"Yes it is. As the old saying goes, 'those who refuse to learn from the past are destined to repeat it.'" She sucked in a harsh breath, chin up. "Not me, Briggs. Not me."

Cody felt absolutely desperate with heartbreak, but he wouldn't beg. He put the bottle down, hoping she didn't notice how badly his hands were shaking.

"We'll talk about it another time. I'll get you back to the hotel in the morning. For tonight you can—"

"No! I have to get back tonight. I have to be there tonight, not tomorrow."

"Look at this storm, Carol," he snapped, pushed to the very limits of his self-control. "The roads'll be rivers. There will be flash floods in all these valleys. Tomorrow's the best I can do."

"But you said it wouldn't last long." She looked up at him in anguish, her blue eyes wide with the first hint of true panic. Tomorrow was the one day she absolutely had to be alone, morning to night. It was *the* day, the single most painful day of her roller-coaster year, the dark valley of her life. The only way to survive it was to adhere to the ritual she'd followed for the last nine years. But there was no way to explain. Licking at dry lips, she could only repeat the words. "No. Tonight. Not tomorrow."

The look on her face frightened Cody. Her pale skin was suddenly so drawn, so tightly stretched across her delicate bones that it threatened to tear apart at the seams. He touched her gently on the shoulder, then tightened his hold to steady her invisible trembling. "Okay, *shicho*. We'll give it an hour after the rain stops, and I'll get you home. Okay?"

She nodded, lips pressed tight against the storm of emotion raging in her breast.

"Here," he said, steering her to the soft leather couch facing the fireplace. "I'll build you a fire, and then I'm going to make you some dinner. Trout okay?"

Carol nodded again. She tucked her feet up under her and leaned back, watching him arrange the logs in the huge stone fireplace. When he had a blaze going, he turned and grinned at her, a flash of boyish charm. "A good fire, a good meal . . . if I open a good bottle of wine, maybe I'll convince you not to run away, Lonesome."

Carol shifted uncomfortably, unwilling to give a promise she knew she could never keep.

Cody shrugged and stood, brushing his hands off on the thighs of his jeans. "Well, you can have the wine anyway, Lonesome. No strings attached. The rest we'll deal with later." Not looking at her, he strode into the kitchen.

FIFTEEN

There was a fax waiting when Carol finally did get back to the Ocotillo around midnight.

From: Jill Stein
            PalmResorts, Atlanta GA

To: Carol Lawson
            PalmResorts, Carefree AZ

    Life offers very few opportunities.
    No guarantees.
    Sometimes you've just got to go for
    it.

    No answer required.

SIXTEEN

October twenty-fifth.

When she was a little girl, the twenty-fifth of any month had made Carol think of Christmas. She was even named after a Christmas tradition: Carols, noels . . . songs of joy. Now the twenty-fifth was filled with sadness.

It had become a ritual, the celebration of this painful anniversary. Up at dawn, she ate no breakfast. She didn't turn on the radio or TV. She wrote a check to The Children's Defense Fund. Then she carefully plotted out the coming year. No mistakes. Caution above all else. Her future in trade for the error of her past.

Something had changed, though, the day before. Cody had changed her. Unbelievable as she would have thought it to be, he had that power, that strange magic. Of course, Jill's friendship had helped, and her own strengths seemed to be resurfacing, buoyant and tenacious. She hadn't thought she had it in her. Though sadness still clung to her, today of all days, within the darkness there was the surprising glow of new hope. Could she honestly forgive herself for her youthful mistake? Could she work as hard for happiness as she did for success and security? Could she trust herself, and life, enough to love this man?

She sat on the couch in her tiny room, and for once she wasn't fighting with her thoughts and feelings. She held each in her mind and studied it with the mixture of confusion and hope one might feel if presented with a chestful of surprises unearthed from a long-buried treasure trove.

Then she grew quiet. It was time.

She took out the pretty little cloth-covered box and held it on her lap. It contained the past, all that she could touch of that lost and painful time. She had done what she thought was best, but that didn't make it the easiest thing to do. She had needed one more reassurance.

It had been her only condition of the adoption. Oh, of course there were all the usual demands: Make them be good people; make them kind; make them loving; make them take good care of the baby. But after that, she had had this one final request: Once a year, a letter to prove that all was well.

So every year, arriving just before this date, a letter came from the adoptive parents.

Nine letters now lay tucked inside the little rosebud-covered box, but she had never opened a single one. She couldn't. It was too painful. There might have been pictures inside, tiny handprints, scrawled crayon drawings. She couldn't bear to sit alone and look at such wonderful things. She couldn't. But just holding the envelopes reassured her. For another year, everything was all right.

Still, she sat on the couch, holding the box between her hands, reluctant to put it back up on the top shelf of her closet. She sat staring at the little pink flowers, remembering little pink toes, little fingers. . . .

The knock on the door made her jump. She didn't expect anyone, certainly not before eight o'clock on a Monday morning. Eyes wide, she stared at the door as if she could see right through it, and suddenly she knew that Cody was standing on the other side. When he knocked again, it was like the beating of her heart against her ribs.

Uncertainty froze her to the spot. "Go away. I can't open the door now."

"I'm not going anywhere. Let me in, Carol."

She stepped up close and pressed her cheek to the door. "I can't, Cody. Please. I don't want company right now."

"I'm not company, Carol. I'm the man who loves you. Open the door, or I'll sit down and camp on your doorstep."

"Briggs, don't be silly now—"

The high, sweet song of a flute fluttered in the morning air, stilling her. Pushing her hair back behind her ears, Carol opened the door.

Cody, leaning casually against the porch rail,

touched two fingers to the brim of his hat. "Mornin',
shicho. I missed you."

She felt her heart leap foolishly in her chest, and
her skin was suddenly warm and damp. Shaking her
head, she took in the sight of him, dark, lean, hard as
flint on the outside but with love shining warm and
sweet in his eyes. Tears rose and her vision shimmered. But she drew in a steadying breath and stood
her ground, blocking the doorway. "I'm serious,
Cody. I want to be alone right now."

"Why now?" he asked softly, his dark eyes skim-
ming her face as he waited for her response. When
she didn't answer, he shifted on his feet. "Want me to
guess, Lonesome?"

She shook her head quickly, afraid he actually
might know. Somehow. Magically. With him, anything seemed possible. "No. It's personal . . . private. Please, Cody, go away."

His broad chest swelled with an indrawn breath,
and he frowned. His rugged face was etched with
lines, his eyes somber. "I respect your privacy, Carol.
And I respect you for being so strong, so determined,
so damn brave. But you were alone nine years ago
today, and I've got no intention of leaving you alone
now. We're one, you and I . . . two halves of a
whole. I can't go away. If you want," he added, stuff-
ing his hands in his pockets, "I'll just sit in a corner
and not say a word all day, but I am coming in."

Stunned, fighting the hot sting of tears, Carol
stepped aside. "Come in then. Shut the door." She
crossed the narrow room and stopped in front of the

alcove that served as her minikitchen. "Can I get you a cup of coffee?"

"If you're having one; otherwise don't bother. I tanked up before I left the ranch."

"Roads any better coming down?" she asked, remembering the deep ruts and gouges the storm had carved.

"Not bad. And the ocotillo's already putting out buds. By this afternoon the whole desert will be in bloom. It's a beautiful sight, *shicho*."

Carol handed him a cup. "It's amazing. I thought there'd be nothing left but devastation."

"Nature's very forgiving," Cody said, looking at her over the rim. His eyes softened. "Coffee's good. Thanks."

With a nod, Carol crossed back to the couch and perched on the edge, tugging the bottom of her shorts down over her thighs. Suddenly, despite the air-conditioning, her T-shirt was sticking to her shoulder blades. Her throat was dry. "You're going to sit quietly in the corner, right?" she demanded, a frown creasing her pale brows.

"If you say so." Cody shrugged, dropping his big body into the nearest chair.

While Carol struggled to find some equilibrium for her chaotic emotions, Cody took a quick survey of the room. "Small but neat. I bet you'd do fine in a hogan."

"A tempting idea." Carol sighed. "I like the Navajo philosophy: Walking on a path of beauty."

"*Biké hojoni*," Cody answered softly. "I like it too.

For me, everything is *hojoni*, the mountains, the desert, the past, the present, and the future . . . and you, Carol. You're part of it now."

Carol squeezed her eyes shut and shook her head in dismay. "You promised, Cody. You said you would sit quietly."

"All right," he said, spreading his hands wide. "Stop trembling so. I'll behave."

"You'd better!" Despite the resolve in her voice, Carol almost felt faint. The room suddenly swam before her eyes. She touched her fingertips to her throat and registered the surprising fact that despite the hot flush washing over her body, her fingers were cold as ice.

In an instant, her hands disappeared into Cody's warm grasp. Kneeling before her, he rubbed her fingers between his palms, then pulled her close against his chest. His warm breath stirred her hair as his lips brushed her cheek. "Are you all right?"

"No. This is so difficult for me."

"I know. But I'm here to make it easier, not add to your hurt. Do you want me to go sit over there?" He gestured over his shoulder. "I'll even go sit back out on the porch, if that's what you want."

Her fingers tightened on the thin cotton stretched across his broad shoulders. "No. Please . . . stay here, Cody. Hold me. Sometimes I feel like I could just blow away and disappear."

"I won't let you. I couldn't live without you." Rocking back on his heels, he studied her with a tender gaze, stunned himself to find how much he loved this woman. One half of his heart, she was; one half of his soul. He ran the back of his fingers down her cheek. "Better now?"

Carol shrugged and forced a shaky smile. "I had this little ceremony, this ritual I've followed for nine years. You've screwed it up completely."

Cody gave a low, husky laugh. "Somehow I don't think I'm sorry."

She touched his face wonderingly. "Somehow I don't think I am either."

Cody moved closer, claiming a seat on the couch right next to her. His knee bumped hers, and without warning the little flower-covered box tumbled to the floor.

Carol reached for it with a stifled cry, then picked it up and held it tightly against her chest, rocking it back and forth, making small moaning sounds. She'd stepped outside herself; all comfort was gone. There was only the box . . . and the terrible grief.

Cody took her into his arms, box and all. He wrapped his embrace around them both, the way he would have those nine years earlier if he had been there. He whispered soft endearments to them both, mother and child. He told her how he wished he *had* been there, wished the past could be rewritten. He offered love now, and promises for the future. Despite the way she sat, so locked away from him in grief, he spoke of the dreams he had.

"Carol?"

At first she didn't answer, but it's strange what love can do. Through the mist and grief came his strong, deep voice; instead of drifting away, she was suddenly anchored in a calm, safe harbor. Love had found her.

Holding his breath, Cody ran his hands up and down her arms, closing his fingers over hers, meshing his hands with hers until they both held the little box. "What's inside, Carol?"

"Inside me or the box?" She smiled softly, the first unqualified smile she'd given in nine years.

Cody's heart stopped. "Both," he said quickly. "Either."

Carol ducked her head, suddenly fearing she was about to fling herself right into his arms and blurt out how much she loved him, how differently she suddenly saw the world. It was almost shyness that held her back. She felt as if she were twenty again, all fresh and new, overwhelmed by the first stirrings of true love. But there was something important to do first. Reluctantly she slipped out of his embrace and stood, holding the box. "Let me put this away, Cody, and then we'll talk."

He stopped her, one strong hand on her arm. "You still haven't told me what's inside."

She shrugged again. The words were difficult to speak. "Letters," she answered. "Every year the adoptive parents have written me a letter. My lawyer sends them on to me. It's always here by the twenty-fifth. Her birthday." She smoothed the top of the box gently with one hand, the way you'd stroke a child's tender head. "I put them away in here. To keep them safe."

"What do they say? Are there any pictures?" Cody's voice was deep and husky with emotion. "What an amazing thing to do," he mused, reaching out to lightly touch the box. "What do they say, Carol?"

Carol stepped back, licking her tongue over suddenly dry lips. "I . . ." She swallowed and tried again. "I don't open them, Cody." Feeling her knees give way, she sank back onto the couch, the box balanced in her lap.

Cody pushed away his dismay and disbelief and searched gently for the right words. "Perhaps you could open them today, with me here by your side."

"I can't," she whispered, tears spilling suddenly down her cheeks.

"Oh, Carol," Cody said softly, taking her into his arms. "You can now. It's all right. Go ahead . . . open your letters."

Her hands toyed for a moment with the lid, stuttering over it the way her words broke apart as she spoke. "I . . . I don't . . . oh, what if . . . oh, I'm afraid!"

"Of course you are. But you're also brave enough to have gone it alone all these years, to have gone through a pregnancy completely alone, with no support, carrying that baby for nine months, feeling her grow, stir to life, worrying about her future. *You did that*. You had that baby, you brought her well and full of promise into the world, and then you were strong enough to grant her a future full of safety and love. You did that, Carol Lawson, you did it all by yourself.

I think you can open the letters now. And this time you're not alone."

She looked at him, more tears balanced on her lower lashes, ready to spill at a blink. "I'm not alone, am I?"

"Not anymore." Cody's dark eyes were wet and glistening too. "Never again."

She drew in a deep, steadying breath and lifted the lid. Inside were the nine letters, different sizes, different color envelopes, but always the same neatly printed return address: 21 Pleasant Lane, Milwaukee, Wisconsin. They had fallen this way and that when the box dropped, and Carol instinctively began to straighten them, making the edges line up so that all nine would lie neatly faceup in a stack.

Cody covered her hand with his. "Why don't you put them in chronological order. Check the postmarks."

When her fingers shook too much to accomplish anything, Cody gently sorted through the letters, arranging them in order. He handed them to her and then waited.

Carol's breath trembled on her lips as she exhaled. A shudder ran through her. Then she felt the reassuring pressure of Cody's hand on her shoulders. She caught her lower lip between her teeth and opened the first letter.

"Dear Carol,
    It surprises me how happy it makes us to write you this letter. Our baby is peacefully

asleep in her crib, and our hearts are overflowing with love for her, and with gratitude to you. She is our joy, our happiness. She is bright and alert, tiny and beautiful, and you can be sure we will do everything in our power to give her a good and happy life. We thank you for giving us this great and wonderful blessing.

We don't know if you'll want to write back, though you are welcome to. Be assured that you'll hear from us once a year and in this way share in the happiness you made possible. God bless you.

> Most fondly,
> Sue and Stuart Burke

P.S. We named her Joy. Joy Carol Burke."

Carol sat absolutely still, her tears dripping onto her lap, her shoulders shaking. She shook her head. "Oh Cody . . . Cody, she's fine and happy! She has a good mommy and daddy. They love her and she's fine, and she'll be safe and well!"

"Yes," Cody answered, wiping his eyes with his fingers. "Yes, she's happy and well, with a family who can care for her and give her a good life. That was the birthday present you gave her, Carol. *You* did that."

Carol dropped her head against his shoulder, wiping her wet face on his shirt, knowing he wouldn't mind. "Let's read the rest."

"Dear Carol,

Here is Joy, all dressed up in her first party dress. We will be celebrating her birthday on Saturday with her grandparents, her aunts, uncles, cousins, and four other one-year-olds from our play group. And you, Carol, will be in our midst, if only in our hearts. . . ."

Carol read through the next six letters, sharing them back and forth with Cody, sometimes remembering to wipe her tears away, sometimes so lost in the wonder of discovery that her tears fell unnoticed. She had not known happiness for nine long years; now it washed over her like a healing balm, over her heart and soul, and she felt as if she were a flower, a tight bud finally opening petal by petal, blooming for the first time. She felt almost like a child herself as she reclaimed those lost years, as she discovered feelings, a world of emotion she'd denied herself all that time. It came like a sweet rain, washing through, gathering power until it was a flood of life-giving happiness . . . joy. Her name was Joy and she was nine years old, happy and well, a beautiful child with soft brown hair, and blue, blue eyes. Joy Carol Burke.

The last letter, the ninth, waited unopened in her hand. She looked at Cody, this wild, dark man, this stranger, this friend, this lover, and smiled through her tears. "I'm almost sorry to have come to the last."

"It won't be the last, *shicho*. There'll be lots more. Every year, more happiness."

"That's a lot to hope for," she whispered, her

hands trembling. It mattered so much. She wanted so much to believe him, to trust him . . . but did she dare?

Cody stared at her, his hands full of letters. There was a war going on behind his dark eyes, between the desire burning through him, and the need to give her time and space to make her own decisions. He wouldn't push her. He'd kept that promise this long . . . he'd endure the torment a little longer. But his inner struggle was painfully evident in the sharp line between his brows, the muscles clenched along his jaw. He ached to promise her anything, *everything*, but he wouldn't push.

Carol looked up into his eyes, into his soul it seemed, and saw the emotions struggling there. They suddenly seemed as easy to read as the letters in her hand. "You know what?" she whispered. "I'm beginning to believe you."

Unfolding the last letter, she smoothed it open on her lap.

"Dear Carol,
After all these years, there is something I want to say, woman to woman. Carol, I hope your life is as filled with happiness and blessings as the life you made possible for us. It was a gift, dear friend I have never met, may never meet, and I thank you for it. I am sure it sometimes caused you pain and sadness . . . even grief perhaps. But I hope those times were few and brief, and eased by love.

As you can see, at nine Joy is quite the tom-
boy, but healthy, happy, and full of spunk.
When she grows up she wants to be a baseball
player, a teacher, a dentist, and a mommy.
Knowing her, it's all possible.
                   Until next year,
              wishing you the best,
                   Sue Burke"

The child smiled up at her from the photo, and
Carol smiled back. She traced the little face with her
fingertip, then tucked the letter into the envelope,
holding the picture aside on her lap. She looked up at
Cody again. "I think I'll buy a little frame and keep
this out."

Cody nodded. "Sounds like a good idea." He
seemed about to say more, but instead he merely nodded again and kept his silence.

Carol pushed aside her nervousness, her newfound
elation, her exhaustion, all the emotions swirling in
fits and snatches through her heart, and struggled to
see past them to the man sitting suddenly so tense and
quiet beside her.

He'd made this happen. He'd ridden to her rescue
like a knight on a white horse. The thought made a
smile twitch at the corner of her lips.

"What are you thinking now, *shicho?*" Cody asked
warily.

Carol tipped her head and studied him with a tiny
smile. "I was just thinking that you rode in and saved
me like the Lone Ranger—"

"Don't!" he ordered, hands tightening into fists as he fought to keep his own emotions under control. "Don't do that, Carol. You want to go from fighting me to putting me up on some pedestal, *anything* to keep from seeing me as the man I am: Your lover, your partner in life. But that's who I am, Carol; that's who I'm going to be."

She looked at him wide-eyed, startled by his vehemence. His intensity was almost anger. It was overwhelming. It left her speechless.

Cody could almost read her mind. Heart pounding in his throat, his muscles aching, he forced himself not to touch her, fought to keep from taking her into his arms and crushing her to his chest. Instead he sat without touching her and looked into her sweet, vulnerable face, her wide blue eyes, afraid that any minute now they'd close against him in fear and caution.

Dammit, he knew he should slow down, hold back, but he couldn't. "I know this frightens you, Carol, and I can understand it. I can sympathize, and console and soothe . . . but that's not enough. Not enough for me, and not enough for us. I love you. It's as simple and as complicated as that. I love you now, and I will love you for the rest of my life and beyond. And you love me, *shicho*. I know you do. But I need you to *tell* me you do. My heart needs to hear those words. My spirit can't soar without them. Trust me, Carol. Let go of the fear and love me, trust me, tell me—"

She rose from the couch and stood for a moment with her back to him, one hand gripping the other so fiercely that her knuckles turned white. Her heart had stopped beating.

He'd risen too, and now she faced him, chin up, her eyes searching his. "You know what you're asking, don't you, Briggs? You're asking me to trust . . . to forgive and forget and trust again, and it's like asking me to stand at the very edge of some terribly high cliff and leap off into nothing—"

"*Not* nothing," Cody insisted, his big body tensing with the need to reassure her, the drumbeat of his heart silenced, waiting. "I know what I'm asking *and* what I'm offering. I'm here; I'll always be here. If you leap, I'll be here to catch you. I won't let you fall. You won't get hurt again, I promise. Oh, Carol, I can't protect you from everything that may happen in life, but I promise to always love you. My love is so strong, it's as though my heart has wings. It's as if . . ." He paused, searching for the word to match the passion that he felt, the one word needed for this moment upon which everything was balanced—past, present, and future. Taking her hand, he pressed her palm against his chest. "Carol, without you my heart is a stone. With you, loving you, my heart is an eagle, soaring free."

The words echoed in the tiny room, and around them swirled the images from Carol's dream. The ruins . . . the high, high cliff . . . the hands reaching out to push her over the edge . . . the eagle soaring into the sky.

And Cody saw them too, the images that had appeared to him in visions, in flashes of symbol cloaked in power and mystery. He knew that place. Shivers walked his skin, lifting the hair at his neck. He'd been right all along; they were one, this woman and he.

Cupping her face in his hands, he smiled into her eyes. "There's a place I want to take you, a secret place, a place of magic. Trust me."

"Yes," she said, touching his face lightly with her fingertips, tracing the dark brow, the rugged jaw. "Yes, I do. I don't know exactly what has happened here, or how, what magic you've worked, what sweet enchantment this is . . . but I do know *this* for certain: I do trust you, Cody Briggs. And I love you."

"That's all I needed to hear. Come—"

"But where?" She gasped, laughing and hurrying to keep up with him as he strode out into the sunlight. "Where are we going?"

"A place you've never been. A place you know."

SEVENTEEN

Carol leaned as far forward as she could against the restraining hold of the seat belt, one hand spread on the dashboard, the other on Cody's warm thigh. She felt as though her heart were flying out ahead of the Range Rover, racing across the desert, leading the way.

Cody grinned at her, his dark eyes drinking in her face, turning to the road ahead only when he had to in order to guide the Rover over the ruts and potholes of a backcountry Arizona road. A golden mesa loomed ahead, and he aimed straight for it, feeling a strange energy flow through him. It grew stronger with each passing mile, like a magnet pulling him . . . like destiny.

He smiled, his beautiful mouth curving up at the corners, his eyes shining. "I told you the desert would be spectacular now, *shicho*. Look at those saguaro, swollen like rain barrels! The ocotillo's got new leaves popping out, and the palo verde too. And look at the wildflowers! Great day to be alive, isn't it?"

"Yes," she said, leaning across the gear shift to kiss his neck just above his shirt collar. "Yes, it is."

She felt it too. Felt the budding of new life all around. Felt the faintest breeze lift from the mesa top. Felt the sun reaching down to touch the two of them with a warm caress. Felt herself floating on happiness as rich and finely woven as some magic carpet.

Then suddenly, shockingly, she felt as if a string were tied around her heart and someone had given it a good sharp tug from the other end. She gasped, pressed a hand to her breast, and leaned forward. Somehow . . . without reason or logic . . . she knew exactly where they were, and where they were going.

"Turn left there," she said, pointing at a rocky outcrop just ahead.

Instead Cody slammed on the brakes. The Rover fishtailed then slid to a stop. His eyes were shining. "What do you mean, 'turn left here?' You don't even know where we're going."

"I do."

"Yes," he answered softly, his eyes locked on hers. "I thought you would. Somehow I *knew* you would."

Carol felt a shiver of excitement wash across her skin. "How?" she whispered. "How can this be? I don't understand."

Cody's smile was a bright arrow of excitement. "Neither do I, *shicho* . . . but I've never questioned the great gifts that life brings. Left turn it is."

They climbed up the side of the mesa along hairpin turns that left Carol's heart pounding. Ahead was a rocky ledge that looked almost like the wall to some ancient ruined castle. She leaned forward again, breathing through parted lips. Waiting. Then there was that tug again. "Go right. There—" She pointed at a seemingly impassable jumble of boulders.

This time Cody merely nodded, eyes narrowed, smiling that same secret smile. He parked at the foot of the boulders and offered her a hand. "No one has come this way for hundreds of years until us . . . me, and now you. I told no one. I didn't trust anyone enough, not even Leonard. But you knew."

She laughed in amazement, started to climb, and missed his last words, words spoken as much to the silence and beauty stretching endlessly around them as to her. "You were always headed here," he said softly. "You were always headed here to me."

Carol was already thirty feet above, climbing up over the round, smooth surfaces of the boulders, aiming for a hidden notch in the wall. She looked at him over her shoulder, her face flushed with excitement, all fear forgotten. "I've been here before. I dreamed it, way back in Georgia before I ever met you, Cody. I dreamed about you. I *think* now it was you. It has to be. Hurry!"

He laughed and followed.

Inside, the ruins lay just as they'd been left a thousand years before. The rooms were empty now, except for an occasional grinding stone, the smaller stone balanced on top. They formed a maze, winding through shadow and sunlight, with dust motes floating in the air like the spirits of those who had loved the place but had to leave. Carol walked into a shaft of golden sunlight and stood, transfixed.

Cody stepped close behind her and circled her with his arms. "Well?" His voice was rough with restrained emotion, but his love shone clear and demanding in his beautiful dark eyes. "Is it me, Carol? Am I the one? Because you are the only one for me."

She drew in a deep, shuddering breath and held it, sorting through the years of her life and placing each behind her, neatly, like stones in a wall, but without another glance. They made a nice, small stack, but nothing compared to the future. Without answering, she laid a hand on his chest. Beneath her palm she felt the heat of him, the fierce pounding of his heart, the astonishing strength . . . and the small metal shape of the amulet he wore. With a soft laugh of delight she tugged it free of his shirt. The eagle glinted silver in the sunlight, sending sparks bouncing off the rocks all around.

She looked up into his eyes, into the love shining in his eyes. "You're the eagle."

He bent his head and nuzzled her cheek. "Am I?"

"Yes," she whispered. "I know it now. All those signs, the dreams . . . Did I tell you I dreamed you? Well, I did. I dreamed I stood here, in this very place, and that old Indian man appeared, dressed in ceremonial robes, and he took the stone out of my heart and placed it here where the past lies peacefully . . . and then he told me about the eagle." She looked up into his dark eyes and smiled. "You're the eagle."

But before he could answer, she danced away, over to the very edge of the mesa where the wall had worn away and there was nothing beyond but the sheer drop down into the canyon.

Cody gave a low, muffled shout of terrible fear and stepped toward her, hands out.

Carol turned, smiling the smile of the safe, the blessed, the loved, and slid her hands into his. "See . . . no one was trying to push me. That was my mistake; all this time, it was my mistake. You weren't trying to push me. You were reaching out to love me."

He gathered her to him, pressing his wet face into her hair. "What am I going to do with you, Lonesome?"

"Well, for one thing, you're going to have to think up a new nickname. Lonesome doesn't suit me anymore." She grinned up at him.

He grinned back at her, then covered her mouth with his. When he came up for air, he was laughing. "And neither will *shicho*; that's a young, *un*married woman."

"Ah . . ." She sighed, kissing his sweet, beautiful mouth. "Then what will you do?"

"Oh, I've already got some ideas I'd like to try out, like 'darling' . . ." One dark brow lifted. "No?"

"Not bad." She smiled, wrapping her arms around his neck. "What else?"

"How about 'dearest'?"

"I like that one."

"I've got one better. I'll call you my wife, my love, and my life."

Carol let the tears roll unchecked down her cheeks. She felt her heart break free and soar, lifted on the wings of happiness. She nodded, losing and then finding herself again in the magic circle of his embrace. "Yes," she whispered, "Yes, Cody. I do love you so, with all my heart, with all my soul."

"As I love you. And we'll spend forever together, you and I, making love, making happiness for each other, making sweet, happy babies. You're going to need a whole lineup of little frames for all the babies . . . if that suits you, Carol?"

"Yes," she whispered, drinking in the sweetness of his kiss. "That suits me just fine."

Cody picked her up in his arms and carried her to a sunlit, sheltered spot where the ground was soft as a feather mattress. They sank down together, wound in each other's arms, their bodies joined as closely as their hearts. They touched and kissed and loved each other right there under the bright blue sky. Then they lay together, too happy to move, stirring only when a shadow crossed the sun. They both looked up to see an eagle soaring above, majestic, wondrous.

Strangely enough, neither one was the least bit surprised.

EPILOGUE

Now you will feel no rain,
    For each of you will be shelter to the other.
Now you will feel no cold,
    For each of you will be warmth to the
        other.
Now there is no loneliness for you,
Now there is no more loneliness,
Now there is no more loneliness.
Now you are two persons
    But there is one life before you.
Go now to your dwelling place
    To enter into the days of your togetherness.
And may your days be good and long upon the
        earth.

APACHE WEDDING BLESSING

THE EDITOR'S CORNER

Escape the summer doldrums with the four new, exciting LOVESWEPT romances available next month. With our authors piloting a whirlwind tour through the jungles of human emotion, everyday experiences take a direct turn into thrill, so prepare to hang on to the edge of your seat!

With her trademark humor and touching emotion, Patt Bucheister crafts an irresistible story of mismatched dreamers surprised and transformed by unexpected love in **WILD IN THE NIGHT**, LOVESWEPT #750. She expects him to be grateful that his office is no longer an impossible mess, but instead adventurer Paul Forge tells efficiency expert Coral Bentley he wants all his junk back exactly where he had left it! When she refuses, little does she realize she is tangling with a renegade who never takes no for an answer, a man of mystery who will issue a challenge that will draw her into the seductive unknown. Hold on while Patt Bucheister skillfully navigates this ride on the unpredictable rapids of romance.

The excitement continues with **CATCH ME IF YOU CAN,** LOVESWEPT #751. In this cat-and-mouse adventure, Victoria Leigh introduces a pair of adversaries who can't resist trying to get the best of each other. Drawn to the fortress by Abigail Roberts's mysterious invitation, Tanner Flynn faces the woman who is his fiercest rival—and vows to explore the heat that still sparks between them! He had awakened her desire years before, then stunned her by refusing to claim her innocence. Join Victoria Leigh on this sexy chase filled with teasing and flirting with utter abandon.

Take one part bad-boy hero, add a feisty redhead, raise the temperature to flame-hot and what you get is a **PAGAN'S PARADISE,** LOVESWEPT #752, from Susan Connell. Jack Stratford is hold-your-breath-handsome, a blue-eyed rogue who knows everyone in San Rafael, but photographer Joanna McCall refuses to believe his warning that she is in danger—except perhaps from his stolen kisses! She isn't looking for a broken heart, just a little adventure . . . until Jack ignites a fire in her blood only he can satisfy. Take a walk on the wild side with Susan Connell as your guide.

In **UP CLOSE AND PERSONAL,** LOVE-SWEPT #753, Diane Pershing weaves a moving tale of survivors who find sweet sanctuary in each other's arms. A master at getting others to reveal their secrets, Evan Stone never lets a woman get close enough to touch the scars that brand his soul. But when small-town mom Chris McConnell dares to confess the sorrows that haunt her, her courage awakens a yearning long-denied in his own heart. A poignant journey of rough and tender love from talented Diane Pershing.

Happy reading!

With warmest wishes,

Beth de Guzman

Shauna Summers

Beth de Guzman   Shauna Summers
Senior Editor   Associate Editor

P.S. Watch for these spectacular Bantam women's fiction titles slated for August: In **BEFORE I WAKE**, Loveswept star Terry Lawrence weaves the beloved fairy tale *Sleeping Beauty* into a story so enthralling it will keep you up long into the night; highly acclaimed author Susan Krinard ventures into outerspace with **STARCROSSED**, a story of a beautiful aristocrat who risks a forbidden love with a dangerously seductive man born of an alien race; *USA Today* bestselling author Patricia Potter follows the success of WANTED and RELENTLESS with **DEFIANT**, another spectacular love story, this time of a dangerous man who discovers the redeeming power of love. See next month's LOVESWEPTs for a preview of these compelling novels. And immediately following this page, look for a preview of the wonderful romances from Bantam that *are available now*!

Don't miss these extraordinary books
by your favorite Bantam authors

On sale in June:

MYSTIQUE
by Amanda Quick

VIOLET
by Jane Feather

MOTHER LOVE
by Judith Henry Wall

HEAVEN SENT
by Pamela Morsi

THE WARLORD
by Elizabeth Elliott

MYSTIQUE

by the *New York Times*
bestselling author
AMANDA QUICK

available in hardcover

*Who better to tell you about this dazzling romance
than the author herself? Here, then, is a personal
letter from Amanda Quick:*

Dear Reader:

Any man who is dangerous enough to become a
living legend is probably best avoided by a sensible,
intelligent lady who has determined to live a quiet,
cloistered life. But sometimes a woman has to work
with what's available. And as it happens, the man they
call Hugh the Relentless is available . . . for a price.

Lady Alice, the heroine of my next book, *Mystique*, does not hesitate to do what must be done. She
requires the services of a strong knight to help her
escape her uncle's clutches; Hugh, on the other hand,
requires assistance in the hunt for a missing gemstone

—and a woman willing to masquerade as his betrothed.

Alice decides that she and this dark legend of a man can do business together. She strikes a bold bargain with him. But you know what they say about the risks of bargaining with the devil . . .

Mystique is the fast-paced tale of a man and a woman who form an alliance, one that puts them on a collision course with passion, danger—and each other. It is the story of a ruthless man who is bent on vengeance and a lady who has her heart set on a studious, contemplative life—a life that definitely does not include a husband.

These two were made for each other.

I hope you will enjoy *Mystique*. When it comes to romance, there is something very special about the medieval setting, don't you think? It was a time that saw the first full flowering of some of the best-loved and most romantic legends, tales that we still enjoy in many forms today. Hugh and Alice are part of that larger-than-life period in history but their story is timeless. When it comes to affairs of the human heart, the era does not really matter. But then, as a reader of romance, you already know that.

Until the next book.

Love,

Amanda Quick

VIOLET

by bestselling author
JANE FEATHER

Sure to continue her spectacular rise to stardom, VIOLET is vintage Jane Feather—passionate, adventurous, and completely enjoyable from the opening paragraph.

"Take off the rest of your clothes."

"What! All of them? In front of you?" She looked outraged, and yet somehow he wasn't convinced by this display of maidenly modesty.

"Yes, all of them," he affirmed evenly. "I doubt even you will take off from the far bank stark naked."

Tamsyn turned away from him and unfastened her skirt. Damn the man for being such a perspicacious bastard.

She dropped the shirt to the ground, loosened the string at the waist of her drawers, and kicked them off.

"Satisfied, Colonel?"

For a moment he ignored the double-edged question that threw a contemptuous challenge. His eyes ran down the lean, taut body that seemed to thrum with energy. He realized that the illusion of fragility came from her diminutive stature; unclothed, she had the compact, smooth-muscled body of an athlete, limber and arrow straight. His gaze lingered on the small, pointed breasts, the slight flare of her hips, the tangle of pale hair at the base of her belly.

It was the most desirable little body. His breath quickened, and his nostrils flared as he fought down the torrent of arousal.

"Perfectly," he drawled. "I find myself perfectly satisfied."

Julian watched as she stood poised above the water. The back view was every bit as arousing as the front, he reflected dreamily. Then she rose on her toes, raised her arms, and dove cleanly into the swift-running river.

He walked to the edge of the bank, waiting for the bright fair head to surface. But there was no sign of La Violette. It was as if she'd dove and disappeared.

He was pulling off his boots, tearing at the buttons of his tunic without conscious decision. He flung his sword belt to the grass, yanked off his britches and his shirt, and dove into the river as close as possible to where he believed his prisoner had gone in.

Tamsyn surfaced on the far side of the rocks as soon as she heard the splash as he entered the water.

She leaped onto the bank, hidden by the rocks from the swimmer on the other side, and shook the water from her body with the vigor of a small dog.

Julian came up for air, numbed with cold, knowing that he shouldn't stay in the water another minute, yet forcing himself to go down for one more look. As he prepared to dive, he glanced toward the bank and saw a pale shadow against the rock, and then it was gone.

His bellow of fury roared through the peaceful early morning on the banks of the Guadiana.

Tamsyn swore to herself and picked up her heels, racing across the flat mossy ground toward the small brush-covered hill.

Julian, however, had been a sprinter in his school days, and his long legs ate up the distance between them.

She fell to her knees with a cry of annoyance that changed to a shriek of alarmed fury as Julian hurled himself forward and his fingers closed over her ankle. She hadn't realized he was that close.

"*Espadachín!*" she threw at him. "I may be a bandit, but you're a brute and a bully, Colonel. Let me up."

"No."

The simple negative stunned her. She stared up into his face that was now as calm and equable as if they were sitting in some drawing room.

Her astonished silence lasted barely a second; then she launched a verbal assault of such richness and variety that the colonel's jaw dropped. She moved seamlessly within three languages, and the insults and oaths would have done an infantryman proud.

"Cease your ranting, girl!" He recovered from his surprise and did the only thing he could think of, bringing his mouth to hers to silence the stream of invective. His grip on her wrists tightened with his fingers on her chin, and his body was heavy on hers as he leaned over her supine figure.

Then everything became confused. There was rage—wild rage—but it was mixed with a different passion, every bit as savage . . .

MOTHER LOVE
by Judith Henry Wall

"Wall keeps you turning the pages."
—San Francisco Chronicle

There is no love as strong or as enduring as the love of a mother for her child. But what if that child commits an act that goes against a woman's deepest beliefs? Is there a limit to a mother's love?

Karen Billingsly's perfect life shatters one night with her son's unexpected return from college. Though neither Chad nor his attorney father will tell Karen what's wrong, she begins to suspect her son has done something unthinkable. And Karen, the perfect wife and mother, must decide just how far a mother will go to protect her son.

Out of habit, Karen ignored the first two rings of the telephone. Phone calls in the night were for Roger—frantic parents of felonious teenagers, wives fearful of estranged husbands, the accused calling from jail, even the dying wanting to execute deathbed wills.

Karen rolled over to his side of the bed and picked up the phone.

It was Chad. She looked at the clock. Not yet five. And instantly, she was sitting up. Awake. Worried.

"Where's Dad?" he asked.

"Padre Island."

"Oh, yeah—the fishing trip. I forgot. That's why you guys aren't coming down tomorrow for the game. When's he coming back?"

"His plane ticket says Sunday morning, but Tropical Storm Clifton is heading their way—and threatening to turn itself into a hurricane. Your father's trying to leave tomorrow instead, but so are lots of other people."

"But you are expecting him tomorrow?" Chad asked.

"I hope so. Are you all right?" Karen half expected him to say he was calling from a police station. Another DUI. Or worse.

"Yeah. Sure. I just wanted you to know I'm on my way home. I didn't want you to think you had a burglar when I come in."

"You're coming home *now*?" Karen asked. "It's awfully early."

He laughed. A thin, tired laugh. "Or awfully late, depending how you look at it. The house had a big party, and I haven't been to bed yet. I need to spend the weekend studying, and with a home football game, this place will be crawling with alums and parents in just a few hours. We're already overflowing with Kansas State guys down for the game. I'll get more done at home."

"Sounds like a good idea. You might even get a home-cooked meal or two."

"That'd be great. Love you, Mom. A lot."

"You sure you're okay?"

"Fine. Go back to sleep."

Karen hung up the phone, curled her body back into its sleep position and closed her eyes. But her mind kept replaying the conversation. Maybe it was from too much beer or the late hour, but Chad's voice had sounded strained—with just a trace of a quiver, like when he used to come padding in the bedroom during a thunderstorm, back when she had been Mommie instead of Mom. "I can't sleep," he would say as he crawled in beside her. And she would curl her body protectively around his and feel him immediately go limp with sleep. She missed that part of motherhood. The physical part. A small, sturdy body pressed next to her own. Plump little arms around her neck. A tender young neck to kiss. She didn't get to touch either of her children enough. With Melissa, it was a pat every now and then, an occasional hug. Chad, after years of adolescent avoidance of his mother's every kiss and touch, now actually reached for her sometimes, but mostly on arrival and departure, not often enough.

She rolled onto her back, then tried her stomach. Her son had sounded worried.

When finally she heard him come in, she went downstairs.

He was standing inside the back door, looking around the kitchen, a backpack and small duffel both hung over one shoulder. He looked almost puzzled, like there was something different about the room. Karen took a quick look around. But it was the same cheerful room it had always been—big round table, captain's chairs, a large braided rug on the brick floor. She slipped her arms around her son who was no longer a boy. He was bigger than his father, more solid. Yet, it was hard to think of him as a man, hard to call him a man.

"Did you and Brenda have a fight?" she asked.

"No," he said, hugging her back, clinging a bit, putting his cheek against her hair. "She's in Tulsa visiting her sister. I'm just feeling shitty from too much beer. Maybe I should have done without the whole fraternity bit—the partying gets out of hand. And some of the brothers are low-life jerks."

"And some of them are nice guys. I can't believe

you're missing a home game," Karen said, relinquishing her hold on him.

"It's only Kansas State. I would have hung around if you and Dad were coming down. But I need to study. And sleep."

"Well, save some time for your sister. She could use a big brother every now and then."

Karen insisted that he take a couple of aspirin with a glass of milk to waylay a hangover. He looked as though the light was already hurting his eyes.

"You want something to eat?"

"No. We had pizza at the party. Two dozen of them."

He followed her up the stairs. She hugged him again outside the door to his room. "It's good to have you home, son. I miss having you around."

"Yeah. I miss you guys, too. Sometimes I wonder why I was in such a hurry to grow up and leave home. I don't have a mom around now to bandage skinned knees and proofread papers."

Karen went back to her bedroom and opened the drapes. The sprawling backyard looked black and white in the hazy first light. Surrealistic even. Like a dreamscape.

She went to the bathroom, then returned to her bed, and sat on the side by the window, staring out at the predawn sky. The weatherman had promised another warm day. Indian summer. Daytime temperatures once again in the upper 80s. Another balmy evening—like last night. Much too warm for a fire in the big stone fireplace in the fraternity house living room.

But her son's clothes had smelled of smoke.

THE WARLORD
by Elizabeth Elliott

"Elizabeth Elliott is an exciting find for romance
readers everywhere."
—*New York Times* bestselling author
Amanda Quick

*Scarred by war and the dark secret of his birth,
Kenric of Montague had no wish for a wife . . . until he beheld the magnificent woman pledged to be his
bride. Yet even as Kenric gave in to his aching hunger to possess her, he vowed she would never tame his
savage heart. But then a treacherous plot threatens
Kenric and his new wife, and now he must fight his
most dangerous battle yet for their lives and for his
soul.*

"Would now be a poor time to ask a question?" Tess
raised her eyebrows hopefully, but the baron's forbidding expression didn't change. Nor did he answer.
Rudeness seemed to be his most dominant trait. Unable to meet his intimidating gaze a moment longer,
she casually turned her attention to the road, ignoring
his silence. "I was wondering what name I should call
you by."

"I am your lord and master, Lady," he finally answered, his tone condescending. "You may address
me as Milord, or Baron, or . . . Husband."

The man's arrogance left Tess speechless. She
considered thanking him—most sarcastically—for al-

lowing her to speak at all, but thought better of the idea. She would behave civilly for the duration of this farce, even if he did not.

"What I meant to ask was your given name, *Husband*. I know your titles, Baron Montague, but I do not know your Christian name."

The man had the audacity to smile at her. Tess quickly dropped her gaze back to the road, half afraid she would betray her anger and smile back. The man was much too appealing by half. That is, when he wasn't being openly rude. Thank goodness he liked to frown. She wasn't at all sure she liked the strange emotions that seemed to befuddle her senses when he didn't look ready to murder her.

"My name is Kenric."

Though her hood was between them, Tess could almost feel his lips against her ear and his breath against her cheek. She marveled at the way his deep voice vibrated right through her body and wondered why the words seemed to steal her breath away.

"You may call me by such whenever we are alone, *Wife*." Kenric expected to get some sort of reaction when he stressed the word 'wife,' but Tess didn't say a word. He pulled her hood aside, surprised to see her smiling.

"You find some humor in my name?" he asked. Her smile grew broader. "Well?"

"Hm?" she inquired absently.

"Why are you smiling?" Kenric demanded, his expression softening when she raised her head and looked up at him. The sweet, faraway look in her eyes was enchanting.

"Your voice," Tess answered dreamily. "I can feel it. Right here." She placed her palm between her breasts, a soft laugh in her voice. "It tickles."

HEAVEN SENT
by Pamela Morsi

*When virtuous Hannah Bunch set out to trap herself
a husband, she hardly dreamed she'd be compromised
by a smoldering, blue-eyed stranger. Her reputation
shattered, she promises to honor and cherish him always—never suspecting that his first touch will spark
an unquenchable flame and his secret will threaten
her life.*

"Violet! Bring me my gun!"

Inside the wellhouse, Hannah Bunch woke from
her warm, pleasant dream, startled to hear the sound
of her father's angry voice. Disoriented at first, she
quickly realized that everything was going as expected. This was a crucial part of her plan, a difficult
part, but one that was essential. Her father would be
understandably angry, she had known that from the
beginning. But it was her father who had taught her
that nothing worth having was achieved without sac-
rifice. A few embarrassing moments could hardly be
counted against a lifetime of contentment.

She knew that more than one couple from the
community had anticipated their wedding night, and
rather than condemning them her father had always
been understanding and forgiving. She had counted
on that spirit of forgiveness, but there was no mercy

in him right now. He was furious and he seemed to Hannah to be talking crazily, directing his anger to the man who stood silently behind her.

"People told me not to trust you, that you're a heathen with no morals, a son of a drunken squaw-man. But I said a man must be judged on his own merits! The more fool me! I invite you into my home, feed you at my table, and this is how you repay me, by ruining my daughter!"

"Papa, please don't be angry," she pleaded, leaving the door of the wellhouse and walking toward her father with her arms outstretched, entreating him. "I love him, Papa, and I think that he loves me," she lied.

Her father's look, if possible, became even more murderous. Her brother, Leroy snorted an obscenity in protest. She grabbed her father's clenched fists and brought them up to her face in supplication. "He's a good man, Papa. You know that as well as I."

The crowd of people stood watching in shock as Violet, who had heard the commotion and her husband's call for a weapon, came running with his old squirrel gun, as though she'd thought some rabid animal had got shut up in the wellhouse. Seeing her stepdaughter, clad only in her thin cotton nightgown, she stood stunned in disbelief, but retained the good sense not to give her husband the weapon.

"Papa, we want to be married," Hannah pleaded, praying silently that Will would not dispute her statement. "Please, we want your blessing."

Her brothers exchanged looks of furious disbelief and righteous indignation.

"You're a dead man!" Rafe, the youngest, threatened.

Hannah was tempted to go over and box his ears.

"Give me that gun!" Ned ordered Violet, but she gripped it tighter.

Hannah's patience with the whole group was wearing thin. It wasn't as if she were a green girl, she was a grown woman of twenty-six and was thoroughly entitled to make her own mistakes.

"I love him, don't you understand?" she lied. "I want to be with him."

"That low-down snake doesn't deserve the likes of you, Miss Hannah!" a voice just to the right of her father shouted in anger. "What's got into you messing with a decent farmer's daughter?" he yelled at the man behind her.

The voice captured Hannah's immediate attention. She turned toward it, shocked. Will Sample, the man she planned to marry, was standing in a group of men staring angrily at the wellhouse.

With a feeling of unreality, Hannah turned toward the object of their anger. In the doorway of the small building, with his hands upraised like a captured bank robber was Henry Lee Watson, a man Hannah barely knew.

And don't miss these electrifying
romances from Bantam Books,
on sale in July:

DEFIANT
by Pat Potter

"A shining talent."
—*Affaire de Coeur*

STARCROSSED
by Susan Krinard

"Susan Krinard has set the standard
for today's fantasy romance."
—*Affaire de Coeur*

BEFORE I WAKE
by Terry Lawrence

"Terry Lawrence makes the sparks
really fly."
—*Romantic Times*

*To enter the sweepstakes outlined below, you must respond by the date specified and
follow all entry instructions published elsewhere in this offer.*

DREAM COME TRUE SWEEPSTAKES

Sweepstakes begins 9/1/94, ends 1/15/96. To qualify for the Early Bird Prize, entry must be received by the date specified elsewhere in this offer. Winners will be selected in random drawings on 2/29/96 by an independent judging organization whose decisions are final. Early Bird winner will be selected in a separate drawing from among all qualifying entries.

Odds of winning determined by total number of entries received. Distribution not to exceed 300 million.

Estimated maximum retail value of prizes: Grand (1) $25,000 (cash alternative $20,000); First (1) $2,000; Second (1) $750; Third (50) $75; Fourth (1,000) $50; Early Bird (1) $5,000. Total prize value: $86,500.

Automobile and travel trailer must be picked up at a local dealer; all other merchandise prizes will be shipped to winners. Awarding of any prize to a minor will require written permission of parent/guardian. If a trip prize is won by a minor, s/he must be accompanied by parent/legal guardian. Trip prizes subject to availability and must be completed within 12 months of date awarded. Blackout dates may apply. Early Bird trip is on a space available basis and does not include port charges, gratuities, optional shore excursions and onboard personal purchases. Prizes are not transferable or redeemable for cash except as specified. No substitution for prizes except as necessary due to unavailability. Travel trailer and/or automobile license and registration fees are winners' responsibility as are any other incidental expenses not specified herein.

Early Bird Prize may not be offered in some presentations of this sweepstakes. Grand through third prize winners will have the option of selecting any prize offered at level won. All prizes will be awarded. Drawing will be held at 204 Center Square Road, Bridgeport, NJ 08014. Winners need not be present. For winners list (available in June, 1996), send a self-addressed, stamped envelope by 1/15/96 to: Dream Come True Winners, P.O. Box 572, Gibbstown, NJ 08027.

THE FOLLOWING APPLIES TO THE SWEEPSTAKES ABOVE:

No purchase necessary. No photocopied or mechanically reproduced entries will be accepted. Not responsible for lost, late, misdirected, damaged, incomplete, illegible, or postage-die mail. Entries become the property of sponsors and will not be returned.

Winner(s) will be notified by mail. Winner(s) may be required to sign and return an affidavit of eligibility/release within 14 days of date on notification or an alternate may be selected. Except where prohibited by law, entry constitutes permission to use of winners' names, hometowns, and likenesses for publicity without additional compensation. Void where prohibited or restricted. All federal, state, provincial, and local laws and regulations apply.

All prize values are in U.S. currency. Presentation of prizes may vary; values at a given prize level will be approximately the same. All taxes are winners' responsibility.

Canadian residents, in order to win, must first correctly answer a time-limited skill testing question administered by mail. Any litigation regarding the conduct and awarding of a prize in this publicity contest by a resident of the province of Quebec may be submitted to the Regie des loteries et courses du Quebec.

Sweepstakes is open to legal residents of the U.S., Canada, and Europe (in those areas where made available) who have received this offer.

Sweepstakes in sponsored by Ventura Associates, 1211 Avenue of the Americas, New York, NY 10036 and presented by independent businesses. Employees of these, their advertising agencies and promotional companies involved in this promotion, and their immediate families, agents, successors, and assignees shall be ineligible to participate in the promotion and shall not be eligible for any prizes covered herein.   SWP 3/95

DON'T MISS THESE FABULOUS
BANTAM WOMEN'S FICTION TITLES

On sale in June

From the blockbuster author of nine consecutive *New York Times* best-
sellers comes a tantalizing tale of a quest for a dazzling crystal.

MYSTIQUE by Amanda Quick

"One of the hottest and most prolific writers in romance today."—USA Today

Available in hardcover ____ 09698-2 $21.95/$24.95 in Canada

VIOLET by Jane Feather

"An author to treasure."—Romantic Times

From the extraordinary pen of Jane Feather, nationally bestselling author of *Valen-
tine*, comes a bewitching tale of a beautiful bandit who's waging a dangerous game
of vengeance—and betting everything on love. ____ 56471-4 $5.50/$6.99

MOTHER LOVE by Judith Henry Wall

"Wall keeps you turning the pages."—San Francisco Chronicle

There is no love as strong or enduring as the love of a mother for her child. But
what if that child commits an act that goes against a woman's deepest beliefs?
Is there a limit to a mother's love? Judith Henry Wall, whose moving stories
and finely drawn characters have earned her critical praise and a devoted read-
ership, has written her most compelling novel yet. ____ 56789-6 $5.99/$7.50

THE WARLORD by Elizabeth Elliott

*"Elizabeth Elliott is an exciting find for romance readers
everywhere . . . . Spirited, sensual, tempestuous romance at its best."*
—New York Times *bestselling author Amanda Quick*

In the bestselling tradition of Teresa Medeiros and Elizabeth Lowell, *The
Warlord* is a magical and captivating tale of a woman who must dare to love
the man she fears the most. ____ 56910-4 $5.50/$6.99
